Summ
Br

MUZZ II:
THE SECRET OF
GOLDTOOTH

by

Jonathan E. Pope

Jonathan E. Pope

Be sure to check out muzzbook.com

This book is dedicated to all the children who read my first book and asked me, "Are you writing another one?"

Also to Mrs. Cindy Stewart and Mrs. Teresa Brumlow, and their 2nd grade classes for all their support and encouragement.

NOTE TO THE READER:

THROUGHOUT THIS BOOK, THERE ARE PROMPTS FROM THE AUTHOR FOR YOU TO EXERCISE YOUR MIND, AND TRY TO SOLVE THE CLUES AND PUZZLES THAT ARE PRESENTED TO THE CREW OF THE LADY ALABAMA... PLEASE DO SO.

ALSO, ANY TIME YOU SEE AN * AFTER A WORD, THIS DENOTES THAT THIS IS AN "ACTUAL THING" AND NOT A "MADE UP THING", AND IT IS THE INTENT OF THIS AUTHOR FOR YOU TO LOOK UP THIS "ACTUAL THING" (IF IT IS UNFAMILIAR TO YOU) TO LEARN MORE ABOUT IT AND BE ABLE TO VISUALIZE IT.

INTRODUCTION

It's still the year 2842. In fact, it's still the same day as the last page of <u>Muzz</u>. If you are now asking yourself the question, "What's <u>Muzz</u>?", then you are way behind. You should probably just go read that book first, or re-read it if you can't remember what happened. But no matter, you should at least know that the Universe is a vast place of 11 galaxies, each having multiple solar systems, each with multiple planets. And it was in Galaxy 9, System 7 that we last saw teenagers Charlie and Lizzie Paige and their new friends: Dr. Addison Fox, a British medical doctor who specializes in Alien Medicine, Captain Jagger Jones, a turtle-man (minus the shell), hot-shot pilot with a Texan/surfer accent, and Marvin, Jagger's co-pilot and master mechanic who is lavender colored, bald, has no visible mouth or eyes, and only speaks in bass tones.

Yet to be more precise, the Paige siblings were on the planet of Tropia, and had entered the Forest of Wimberlies, home to the Muzz Bugs.

CHAPTER 1

THE NEWS

Whoosh! The white feathery seedlings flew up from behind the flying motorbikes that Charlie and Lizzie Paige rode on as they sped through the magnificent forest of giant dandelions. This time around, Lizzie was not intent on winning a race, but instead she was more interested in taking in the beauty of her surroundings. For Charlie, it was now his second trip into the heart of the Forest of Wimberlies, and he felt like an expert tour guide to his little sister. He pointed out the foot wide, navy blue ladybug-like creatures with the yellow zig zag pattern on their backs.

"That's them," he called out. "Those are the Muzz Bugs."

As they flew toward the heart of the forest, the concentration of Muzz Bugs grew, just as Charlie had remembered. Some flew, some walked, some clung to the trunks of the massive silver dandelions. He continued to tell his sister all he had learned about the unique species over the last few days. Then they saw the large stalked wimberly with its chevron pattern markings. He advised Lizzie to slow her bike, and then to stop. They dismounted their fliers and stood next to each other as a breeze began to blow.

The wind increased. Charlie leaned toward his sister and said, "Watch this."

As he'd seen before, the mass of Muzz Bugs grew, dipped down into a bowl formation, then from the center, the formation rose with the queen seated at the pinnacle. Charlie glanced over at Lizzie whose jaw dropped and eyes glistened with wonder. The formation lowered and the queen was brought slightly above the height of the two teenagers.

Charlie reached over and grabbed his sister's hand and said, "Queen Lizzie, I would like you to meet my sister, Lizzie." The teenage girl curtsied to the Muzz Bug who wore a tiny tiara and whose yellow pattern sparkled in a way that none of the other bugs' did.

"Well," started Queen Lizzie, "I guess it is safe to say that your quest was successful. Oh, and what a lovely girl she is... a beautiful girl to match her beautiful name," and Queen Lizzie winked at Lizzie Paige, who blushed and smiled. "And our deal? I take it you told no one of your discovery?" the queen continued.

"No ma'am," replied Charlie. "Not a soul. Nor did any of the other crew. The secret is safe with us, your highness, and you'll be happy to know that all clues are still in place."

"Well done, young man. I never doubted you."

"And ma'am," started Lizzie, "I just wanted to tell you how very grateful I am to you for your part in all this. Charlie tells me he could not have done it without your cooperation... so, well, ma'am," she kind of stuttered, "well, thank you. Thank you so much for... well, for caring enough."

The queen smiled and began to reply, when she was interrupted, which caught her off guard because she knew no one there would dare interrupt her. But, the interruption did not come from anyone there... it came from Jagger who was back at the Lady Alabama with Marvin and Dr. Fox.

"Charlie?" the voice came in over one of the bike's speakers. "Hey Chuck, you there?"

Charlie looked at the queen first. She nodded her permission and he quickly stepped back to his bike and touched a button, "Yeah," he replied, "We are speaking with the queen. What's up?"

"Charlie," the voice had now changed to that of Addison, and it had a tone of concern, "we just received a radio news broadcast from Galaxy 4. It seems a cruise ship there has gone missing, and well, I couldn't help but remember that you said…"

"Mom and dad!" interrupted Lizzie.

"What did it say?" asked Charlie holding back panic. "Did it say what happened to the ship?"

"No," replied Addison, "only that it had vanished. The news reporter said it was quite a mystery. He said 'thus far there were no leads as to what had happened to the ship.' "

Charlie trying to hold onto hope asked, "Did they give the name of the ship? There easily could have been more than one cruise ship in Galaxy 4 at the time."

There was a pause on the other end of the radio. Then Addison's voice returned, "They did. They said it was the Saint Louis the Lionhearted that left from Earth last week."

Lizzie and Charlie's hearts sunk when they heard this news. That was indeed the ship their parents were on.

There was silence for quite a few moments, but the silence was broken by the voice of Queen Lizzie, "WELL, it looks like the two of you have another quest to go on. AND, it sounds like it could be dangerous. SO, I would like to offer my head of security, Benny, to go with you. Benny is a Muzz Bug of great talents and could be of great use to you on this mission."

As she spoke, a Muzz Bug from behind her came forward. He was wearing tiny black sunglasses, and with a macho yet monotone voice, Benny the Muzz Bug said, "At your service."

They were not sure how Benny could help them, but Charlie and Lizzie did not feel they were in any position to turn down an offer from the queen. Plus, they really weren't sure what lay ahead.

They thanked the queen again and once more mounted the flying motorbikes. As fast as they could, they flew back through the forest toward the Lady Alabama. Benny gathered a few things and strapped a small satchel around himself, and after the two teens had a couple minutes head start, he flew after them.

Chapter 2

The Return to Aviotto

When Charlie and Lizzie got back to the outer edge of the forest, they saw Benny the Muzz Bug entering the Lady Alabama with his small bag. As they pulled up to the ship, Jagger and Addison walked over to the teens to greet and comfort them.

"That's Benny," Charlie said pointing to the Muzz Bug entering the space craft. "The queen is sending him with us."

"Yeah, he filled us in," said Jagger. "He got here about five minutes ago. Seems like a ball of laughs," Jagger remarked sarcastically.

"Five minutes?" Charlie asked confused. He knew they had quite the head start on the little fellow and had flown as fast as they could back to the ship. "Five minutes," he repeated this time with a tone of impressed respect.

"So I was thinking," said Dr. Fox, but before she could finish her thought, Charlie blurted out, "We need the professor. We need to go back to Aviotto."

He quickly realized that he had just been quite rude and interrupted Addison. "I'm sorry, Dr. Fox. What were you saying?"

She began again, "I was going to say that I think we need the professor and we should head back to Aviotto." She smiled at Charlie, and he returned a smile back to her.

"Well alright then," Jagger clapped his hands together once, "I guess it's time we get this party started." The four of them boarded the Lady and were quickly headed back to the bird planet of Aviotto.

When they arrived to Aviotto, Jagger landed the ship in the same spot they'd parked it the previous two times. The crew left the ship and walked to the "elevator tree". Once there, they realized that without Professor Hootie, they had no way of opening the elevator door which they had used on their first trip to Aviotto to ascend up into the treetop village known as Owlville. They showed Benny which branch should be pulled down in order to open the tree's door, but he flew to it and was not heavy or strong enough to cause the branch to budge.

"Maybe you guys just stay here and I'll go ask around?" Benny said in his dry, monotone voice as he looked upward to the village in the large sequoia trees*. "You said this guy's name is Hootie?"

"Professor P. Gordon Hootie," answered Addison, "He's likely with a woman named Darla."

"Roger that. Gordon and Darla. I'll be back momentarily," and with that, Benny jetted up into the treetops leaving the rest of the crew behind.

"That bug is all business," stated Jagger as they watched Benny fly away.

About 8 minutes later Benny returned and said, "I could not find Gordon and Darla, but I talked to a couple of locals who seemed to know them. They said they had gone to a place called Egret Gardens about thirty miles from here. My intuition says I shouldn't trust a couple of do-dos like those two oafs, but it's my only lead."

Charlie, Addison, and Jagger almost simultaneously said, "Burt and Curt," and Marvin held his belly and shook like he was laughing, but no sound was made.

"You know these two?" enquired Benny.

"Yes," stated Addison, "And I'm sure they are telling the truth."

Meanwhile, thirty miles north of Owlville, Professor Hootie and Darla sat cozily on a picnic blanket which sat on top of the most beautiful grass you've ever seen. They were in the middle of a circle of giant, five foot tall tulips* that ran forty rows deep; four rows of yellow tulips, then 4 rows of pink, then four rows of orange. Each bloom the size of a normal person's head. The pattern of tulips was like a giant bullseye and the professor and Darla were smack dab in the center.

At this point, it had been about 14 hours since the professor had been dropped off on his home planet.

"Did you miss me, Gordon?" asked Darla.

The professor ate a spoonful of a steaming bowl of soup that Darla had poured from a thermos. "Mm, mm," said the professor, "I sure missed this home cooking. I haven't had a meal this good in years. What is it?"

"Cream of regurgitated rodent soup," said Darla quickly, and then she sulked a bit at Professor Hootie's obvious avoidance to her question.

The professor got the hint and quickly fixed the situation, "Oh, come on Darla, you know I did. I bet I thought about you at some point everyday."

"For twenty-five years?" she said in disbelief. "Then why didn't you come home sooner?"

"Well, I… I…" the professor stuttered, " I don't really know. I love teaching and I… well, I… I think I was supposed to be there… for Charlie… for Lizzie. But I'm here now. Now it's just me and you

Darla. Oh, Darla I hope to make up for lost time. I want it to be just you and me from now on. Yes," it was like a light bulb went off in the professor's head and from the glowing look on Darla's face it was like she could read his mind. "Yes," he continued, "we should get m…" he stuttered again. Darla smiled and nodded, as if to say "go on", her eyes sparkled with joy.

"We should get m…" the professor paused. He had been gazing into Darla's eyes, but now, just for a second his gaze wandered up toward the sky.

Darla, about to explode with excitement spoke up, "Go ahead, Gordon, 'we should get…"

"A Muzz Bug?" the professor finished, and Darla's face collapsed with disappointment and confusion all at once.

"Why should we get a Muzz Bug?" she asked perplexed.

"What?" asked the professor, not moving his stare from the sky, then realizing what Darla had asked. "No, no. We shouldn't get a Muzz Bug… look there," and he stood and pointed into the air. Darla turned from her seated position, pulled her left wing hand up to shield the sun, and saw a small figure flying toward them. It was obviously not a bird.

"What in the dickens?" exclaimed the professor, as the Muzz Bug had gotten close enough for him to now make out the creature's tiny sunglasses.

The Muzz Bug's thin wings were moving so fast that you could barely see them, and he appeared to just hover. Both Professor Hootie and Darla were completely caught off guard by this most unexpected visitor. Benny gently landed on the top of a large yellow tulip.

"Are you P. Gordon Hootie?" asked Benny in his all-business-like tone.

"Indeed I am," replied the professor. "And whom might you be?"

"I'm Benny, sir. Head of security for Queen Lizzie Arelius of the planet Tropia."

"Yes, I know the queen. I spoke with her only a few days ago," replied Professor Hootie.

"Roger that, sir. I was there. Anyway, sir, your service is requested for a rescue mission."

"A rescue mission?"

"Affirmative."

"For whom? Where? Who sent you? The queen?"

"Not exactly, sir. I was sent to retrieve you by Mr. and Miss Paige," replied Benny.

"Charlie and Lizzie? But a rescue mission? We already saved her."

"It's not Lizzie, sir. It's their parents. The cruise ship they are on has gone missing," Benny paused like he'd just realized something, then continued, "I guess you could say it's a 'search and rescue'."

A concerned look came across the professor's face. He then turned to Darla, and without saying a thing, Darla could tell that he was asking for permission.

"Go," she said. "Help them find their parents. I'll be here." She sighed, "I've waited twenty-five years, I think I can wait a little bit longer."

The professor leaned in and kissed Darla on the cheek, then without saying anything took off into the air flying in the direction that Benny the Muzz Bug had flown in from.

Benny delayed, looked at Darla and said, "It's been a pleasure, ma'am." Then, he also took off into the air and quickly passed Professor Hootie, leading him back to the Lady Alabama.

Chapter 3

Searching Galaxy 4

Everyone greeted the professor warmly but briefly, (I mean, it HAD been less than a day since they'd seen him) and they quickly boarded the ship and left Aviotto.

"Alright," started Professor Hootie, "someone fill me in. Where was the cruise ship last seen?"

Dr. Fox began, "According to the radio report, the last communication from the ship came as they were leaving Cyfos."

"That's Galaxy 4, System 2," Jagger chimed in.

"So what are the authorities saying?" asked the professor.

"Not much," replied Addison. "They haven't found anything in two days of searching and have deemed it to be a..." she paused because she knew Charlie and Lizzie did not want to hear this piece of information, which she and Jagger had omitted from telling them previously. She continued, "Since there are no traces of the ship, they suspect a star bomb was detonated on the ship itself. They have officially called off the search." She immediately saw the disappointment on the faces of Charlie and Lizzie.

"After only two days? Imbeciles!" The professor had also seen the looks on the teens' faces. "Jagger, let's get to Galaxy 4, System 2. Marvin, see if you can find out where the ship was headed after Cyfos. We'll get this situation figured out, and we'll find your parents, kiddos," he said with great confidence.

Charlie and Lizzie perked up a bit, and took their seats for the flight, as did the other crew members. Jagger and Marvin put on their sunglasses, Benny always wore his, and the other four found some shades as well. Then, Jagger gave out a great big, "Giddy up!" and a bright light came rushing through the windshield of the ship.

It took ten and a half hours to travel from Galaxy 9, System 7 to Galaxy 4, System 2. The crew (except for Marvin) slept for most of the trip. It had been a long few days. As they entered the system, they flew towards Cyfos. There were only six planets in Galaxy 4, System 2, and the planets were a bit more spread out than they had been in Galaxy 9, System 7 where there were twenty-two planets.

The professor asked, "Marvin, any word on which planet the cruise ship was headed to after Cyfos?"

Marvin nodded, made a couple of quick motions with his hands, and the itinerary for the St. Louis the Lionhearted cruise liner appeared in the middle of Lady Alabama's cabin.

It read: "Day 12-13 dock at Cyfos, Day 14-15 travel to Funchess, Day 16-17 dock at Funchess."

"So let's start at Cyfos and head toward Funchess," stated Charlie.

"I agree," remarked the professor. "Maybe something will turn up."

Jagger did just that. They flew slower than Charlie was used to. He had been so used to speeding from one planet to the next, that this taking their time and looking carefully for any sign of clues was very different to him, and honestly a bit boring. There was nothing but space for as far as their eyes could see.

After hours of flying at what felt like a snail's pace and seeing virtually nothing, Charlie began to understand why the authorities had given up after two days. Even though he had no thoughts of giving up, the question did go through his head, "Did a star bomb go off and the entire ship disintegrated into the nothingness of space?" He sure hoped not.

Jagger was getting quite bored as well. He could almost feel the troubling thoughts and doubts creeping into the siblings' minds, when he spotted a small asteroid field a bit to the right of their course.

"Hey, Chuck," he said, "you up for a little detour? I could show you something cool about Lady here that you haven't gotten to see yet."

Charlie looked over at Marvin who was squirming in his seat with excitement.

"How much time are we talking?" asked Charlie.

"Thirty minutes, tops," replied Jagger.

Charlie looked over at Lizzie to get her thoughts.

"I'm fine with it, B.B. We're less than an hour from Funchess and we've got no clues so far," stated Lizzie.

"Let's do it," Charlie directed toward Jagger. "Show me what she's got."

Marvin began beating on his chest, and Jagger steered the ship off course toward the asteroid field. When they had reached it Jagger said to Marvin, "Little buddy, load the potato gun!"

"The potato gun?" asked Charlie.

"That's what I call Lady Alabama's laser cannon. It sounds more friendly. Don't you think?"

Charlie just chuckled and shook his head.

"Wait," Benny chimed in, "Are we about to blast an asteroid with a laser cannon?" he asked.

"Affirmative," Jagger answered, doing his best impression of the stoic little Muzz Bug.

"Awesome," replied Benny quietly.

Jagger smiled at the "normal" comment by the Muzz Bug, then asked Marvin, "Is our spud ready for launching?"

Marvin gave him a thumbs up, then on the holographic screen in front of him pulled up an image of the asteroid field. He drew a circle around one of the asteroids with his index finger, then made his hand into the shape of a gun, and fired it. When he did, a laser blasted from underneath the ship and hit one of the asteroids square in the center sending rock debris flying in all directions. The entire crew was impressed, but especially Benny.

"Can we do another one?" he asked.

Jagger grinned and said, "Hit it, Marvin." Marvin started up the bass sounds, "Nnt, nnt, nnt," and scanned the field on his monitor. He picked one at the edge of the field, circled it, and pulled his trigger. Boom! Another direct hit with asteroid shrapnel sent flying. Everyone cheered, and once again Benny seemed most impressed.

"That…was…AWESOME!" he announced loudly, catching the rest of the crew off guard. He quickly seemed to realize he was acting out of character, and tried to recompose himself. "Sorry," he said quietly and calmly, "I'm sorry. It's just… well… I've never really seen anything blow up before and it was quite exhilarating, I must say."

There was an awkward silence, which was broken by Jagger saying, "Well, okay. I think it's time to get this puppy turned back around."

Jagger began to turn the ship back toward their course when, all of a sudden, Lizzie shouted, "What is that?"

Chapter 4

Puddles

Lizzie pointed to an area where some rock debris had been sent flying, and it seemed to create a ripple effect in space as if someone had just thrown a pebble into a pond. The other crew members eased toward the front of the cabin close to the windshield.

"Do you see it?" Lizzie asked.

"I see it," replied Charlie, "but what *is* it?"

Simultaneously Professor Hootie and Jagger uttered the same words, "A puddle."

Marvin slapped his hands against the side of his face and shook his head in disbelief. The rest of the crew just looked confused.

"So, what's 'a puddle'?" Charlie asked.

"Well," started the professor, "puddles are…" he paused to try to figure out the best possible way to explain this strange phenomenon. "Puddles are portals. They are like cousins of black holes. Like wormholes that are portals to other places."

"To where?" asked Lizzie.

"Well, that's the problem," responded Professor Hootie, "no one really knows."

"They're dangerous," Jagger chimed in.

"How so?" asked Charlie.

"It throws your compass out of whack. Knocks out your entire guidance system… puddle jumping, that is."

"Puddle jumping?" Lizzie asked.

"That's what it's called to go through one," responded the professor. "Puddle jumping."

"Have you ever done it?" Charlie asked the professor.

"Oh no. No, no," answered the professor.

"I have," Jagger said in a tone that was the most serious any of them had ever heard him use. Everyone's focus turned toward the turtle-man. Charlie felt like he was a kid around a campfire about to listen to a ghost story.

"It was about fifteen years ago. I was... well... let's just say I had made a mistake, and some people were wanting to punish me for that mistake, and I was trying to lose them... but I couldn't. That was way before I got Lady here, or before I'd even met Marvin. At that time I was flying a little craft called Bella Tonna. Bella wasn't nearly as fast as Lady here. Well, anyway, I was in Galaxy 7, System 3 and I was trying to shake these guys, and they were shooting at me and Bella, when all of a sudden I see ripples form out ahead of me after one of their star torpedos misses me and explodes. It was a puddle. I had heard of 'em...

never actually seen one, but I'd heard stories, in flight school and what-not. Well, I figured my best chance to lose those guys was to puddle jump, so I did. I flew ol' Bella right into the thing. Her compass went nuts. Everything related to guidance on the whole ship, just went caput, and I came out the other side and I had no idea where I was. I spent 3 weeks flying around not knowing where I was or where I was headed. For awhile I questioned whether I was in the known universe. I had to ration food and supplies, and was all by myself. I just about went crazy, and felt sure I was going to die out there just flying to nowhere." He paused.

Lizzie, completely engrossed in Jagger's story, chirped up with anxious anticipation, "So what happened?"

"So three weeks in, and I'm losing it, right? And I finally see them. Two planets, almost side by side. It was Castor and Pollux, the twin planets. I was in Galaxy 10, System 4. System 4 of Galaxy 10 is a big system, area wise. Very big. One of the biggest. BUT, there are only TWO planets in the entire system and they happen to sit right next to each other. Until I saw those fellas, I had no clue where I was."

"Well," stated Charlie, "this time we have each other. I say we do it. We HAVE to puddle jump. They searched this area for two days and found no traces of the cruise ship our parents were on. I'm thinking the ship MUST have gone into the puddle."

"But Chuck," said Jagger, "we had to travel well off course to get over here to the puddle. The cruise ship would have had no reason to veer that far off course."

"Well," Charlie paused trying to think of a scenario that might be plausible, "well, what if they were taken off course, by somebody, or some thing?"

This statement caused Jagger and Professor Hootie to stand up a little straighter, and realize that Charlie might be on to something. It was something that caused both of them great concern, and just as they had done earlier, they spoke the same word in unison.

"Pirates."

Also as *he* had done earlier, Marvin threw both his hands up to where they smacked the side of his lavender face, and he slowly shook his head.

CHAPTER 5

PIRATES AND THE T.U.S.K.

"Pirates?" questioned Charlie. "Like eye patches and plank walking pirates?"

"Well...kind of. I mean they are space pirates, but honestly I've met a few with eye patches," stated Jagger.

"There are quite a few bands of pirates that roam the universe," Professor Hootie informed them. "Most are bands that have been around for many years, but every now and then you hear about a new group that has popped up somewhere. Some groups of pirates are all the same species, from the same planet. Others are made up of multiple species, from multiple planets. Most stick to pirating their own system, but I guess that's the thing about pirates…they really don't follow any set rules."

"But Doc," said Jagger, "here's the thing I'm struggling with, all the pirates I've ever known were too scared to puddle jump because of its randomness. I mean, seems like pretty good luck to jump right where a cruise liner is."

"Indeed," agreed the professor. "But what if puddles weren't random? What if they knew to which galaxy, and to which system they would be jumping to?"

Dr. Fox chimed in, "Then they could use the puddles as planned get-away routes that no one would know about."

"Indeed," agreed the professor.

"Yeah, but," Jagger began, "I've always been told they were random. Do you know something I don't?"

"Legend says…" started the professor, but Charlie quickly interrupted.

"Seriously, another legend?"

Professor Hootie grinned and winked at the teen, "There was once an elite secret society called the T.U.S.K., which stood for The Universe's Secret Keepers."

He was interrupted again, this time by Lizzie, "It's quite redundant isn't it?"

"What my dear?"

"I mean calling themselves 'THE T.U.S.K.' It's like saying The The Universe's Secret Keepers."

The professor was almost embarrassed that he'd never thought of that, but then smiled and said, "Why, you make a good point, my dear. Indeed it is. Quite redundant."

"So tell us more about these secret guys who kept secrets," implored Charlie.

"Well the T.U.S.K. was supposedly made up of some of the brightest engineers, astronomers, mathematicians, historians, physicists, chemists, and other scientists in the universe. But, about 200 years ago, the T.U.S.K. members thought themselves so elite that they never let any new members in. Eventually the last member of the T.U.S.K. died, and with him, all the secrets kept by the T.U.S.K. There were many secrets that were thought to have gone to the grave with the last member of the T.U.S.K. and one of them was the location of all the puddles in the universe and knowledge of which system you would enter if you puddle jumped. If this legend is true, and someone else now knows this secret, then maybe they are using the puddles as 'get-away routes' as Addison so delicately put it."

"Interesting," Jagger commented.

"I have to admit," continued the professor, "it has always been a bit of a fantasy of mine to revitalize the T.U.S.K."

"I couldn't think of a better person to do it," said Addison.

"And hey," Charlie interjected, "you know where the Muzz Bug anti-venom is and I bet none of the T.U.S.K.'s knew THAT secret." This comment drew a laugh from the rest of the crew.

Then Lizzie said, "But if you do, restart the group, I'd drop the 'THE'. You wouldn't want to be redundant."

They all laughed again and Dr. Hootie replied, "Indeed."

When the laughter stopped, Charlie spoke up again with a serious tone, "You know I'm right though, right? You know we have to go through?"

Jagger and Professor Hootie looked at each with concern, but in agreement with Charlie. Then Jagger turned to Benny and said, "How bout you, little dude, you got any thoughts on the situation?"

Benny quickly replied, "I am here to help these two find their parents, and if that means flying through a mysterious, rippling portal in space, then so be it."

"Well," started Jagger, "I guess we have our answer."

He was then interrupted by Benny once more, who said, "And if we have to blow up something else along the way… so be that, too."

"Easy there, cowboy. Let's just see where this puddle takes us for now," retorted Jagger. "You guys might want to take your seats again," he announced, and he eased the Lady Alabama to the edge of the puddle. The tip of her nose rested a foot away from the rippling surface. Jagger sighed, and with much less enthusiasm than he'd used since Charlie had known him, Jagger said quietly, "Giddy-up."

And they entered the puddle.

CHAPTER 6

PUDDLE JUMPING

Blackness was all that could be seen through the front of the ship's windshield. There were no stars, no planets; nothing that could be seen. Then the internal lights of the ship went out, and their engine cut off. All the hums and vibrations from all electrical components of the ship ceased without any aid from the crew. Once the Lady Alabama was completely engulfed in the puddle, there was only darkness, silence, and stillness as the ship stopped moving forward. This lasted for ten seconds; just long enough for the crew to feel the eeriness of the nothingness. Then, all of a sudden, without warning or logical explanation, the ship began to free fall. It was like gravity had been turned on with the flip of a switch. The crew screamed a scream like you'd hear at an amusement park from people on a scary ride. Well, all of the crew except for Marvin, of course. He had his hands raised in the air like he was riding a fun rollercoaster.

After they felt they had fallen hundreds of feet in a matter of seconds, the ship stopped falling, but was now almost sliding as if through a pipe. The darkness was replaced by beautiful colored light of swirling pinks and purples and yellows and turquoise. It was like a tie-dyed explosion of light. They slid down and to the right, then the left, over a hump, back to the right and then swirled down as if spinning around the inside of a large toilet bowl and… pop. They were shot out and back into space, with the Lady's engines back on and slowly moving forward, just as they had been when they entered the puddle. The entire event had taken only thirty seconds.

The crew appeared completely disheveled, hair all out of place, catching their breath, no one saying a word for at least another thirty seconds. Then, Jagger finally spoke up, "Did I forget to mention that part?"

They all quickly glared at him spitefully, except for Benny who quietly spoke, "Again, can I say," and he crescendoed, "that wAS AWESOME! This may be the greatest day of my life."

Everyone burst into a relieved laughter, and Marvin held his belly with both his hands and shook in his co-pilot's chair.

"So," asked Charlie looking at the guidance screens and realizing the ship's navigation systems were indeed thrown out of whack inside the puddle, "where do we think we are?"

The crew gathered near the windshield and surveyed their surroundings. Three planets could be seen. The closest was a bright orange planet with small green circles that almost looked like polka dots from the distance. It looked a bit like Earth except orange instead of blue, with no clouds, and less green. It had two moons; one pale yellow moon, and one smaller baby blue moon which seemed to almost be more of a moon to the yellow moon, instead of the planet.

In the distance, to the right of the orange planet, they could see a grayish planet with a series of purple rings of different intensities. At around the same distance from the orange planet, but to its left, was a light green planet with darker green spots, much like the orange planet in front of them. Jagger spun the ship around to see a blue cored sun with a yellow halo burning behind them.

He then spun the ship back to face the orange planet once more.

"Well, captain, what do you think?" Professor Hootie asked Jagger.

"Blue sun... could be a number of different systems. That orange planet, though... with those moons... only two possibilities I think."

"Which are?" prodded the professor.

"Well, Dadbross in Galaxy 2, System 3, or Elenarrus in..." he paused to think.

"Let's see if playing that game in that arcade has paid off for you," stated the professor.

"Galaxy 6, System 1," Jagger quickly blurted out with a big grin on his face.

"Well done," said the professor also grinning.

"So which is it, are we in Galaxy 2 or 6?" Lizzie inquired.

"Six," stated Jagger with confidence. Then second guessing himself, he looked at the professor for backup and said with much less confidence, "I think we're in Galaxy 6?"

Professor Hootie nodded, "I believe this to be the case as well. That gray planet with the purple rings I believe is the planet Welch and that green one is almost certainly Vivivikin, both of which are neighbors to Elenarrus."

"So should we go to Elenarrus, or one of the others?" asked Dr. Fox.

"My gut says Elenarrus," replied the professor. "Remember the group I just told you all about?"

"The The Universe's Secret Keepers?" replied Lizzie with a smirk.

"Yes, the T.U.S.K. That's the one. Well, from research I did on them about seven years ago, I have reason to believe that Elenarrus is the planet where they met. I even believe that the planet was named by members of the T.U.S.K.," stated the professor.

"Okay, I'll bite," Benny said dryly. "What brings you to that conclusion?"

"Well, the T.U.S.K. likes to leave little hints, clues if you will, around the universe. It's their way of creating more secrets for themselves to keep. Anyway, if you pay attention, you can pick up on those little hints, like the name of the planet, Elenarrus." He paused to see if anyone had seen it yet. When he realized they had not, he said it slower, "Ele-Nar-Rus. There are relatively few animals that actually have tusks, not horns, but actual tusks. Anyone want to take a guess at three of those animals?"

And like a lightbulb had come on and crashed into their heads, the entire crew almost in unison said, "Ooooh."

Then Benny quickly said, "Wait, I don't get it."

Charlie jumped in, "The name… Elenarrus… it's just a melding of the names of three animals that all have tusks; an elephant, a narwhal*, and a walrus."

"Yeah," Benny said feeling embarrassed he had not seen it earlier, "yeah, that's what I was thinking. I just," he stuttered, "I just wanted to make sure that's what you guys were thinking… an elephant, a walrus, and a narwhal." Then, under his breath, he muttered, "Whatever that is."

"To Elenarrus!" Charlie exclaimed.

"To Elenarrus!" the rest of the crew repeated.

CHAPTER 7

THE MAN IN THE WHITE HAT

They took the most direct path possible through the atmosphere of Elenarrus which Charlie and Lizzie now realized was a much smaller planet than Earth. As they flew down they saw an ocean of orange water with waves crashing around. They could also now see that the green polka dots they'd seen from space, were actually islands of lush green jungles. And, as they neared the closest island, a shape began to come into focus that they could not believe.

It was a massive cruise ship. It was floating in the water near the island that was closest to them. Charlie, Lizzie, and the rest of the crew held their breath as they flew close enough to read the side of the massive cruise liner… "St. Louis the Lionhearted" it read. And the crew erupted with excitement. They knew that was the ship that the Paiges had left on; the ship that had vanished; and now here it was. Charlie and Lizzie would be reunited with their parents momentarily.

Jagger flew above an empty deck at the highest part of the ship and hovered close to it. Charlie, Lizzie, Addison, Professor Hootie, and Benny all climbed into the airlock in the floor of the ship. The door above them closed and the one below them opened and they fell only a few feet onto the ship's deck.

As they gathered themselves, and before they had even figured out where to go next, they were greeted, "Hello there," came a friendly voice, "are you the rescue party?"

They saw a man in a navy and gold cruise liner uniform. He had on a white hat with a wide bill that was turned up in the back and progressively came down in the front creating a point. He walked slowly toward them, and crowds of people began to appear behind him.

Dr. Fox spoke first, "Well, maybe… sort of."

The man looked confused.

"Are you the captain of this ship," asked Professor Hootie.

"No," the man answered, "I'm a 'co-pilot' although really more of an 'events coordinator'. I've never really flown a ship like this before. Never thought I'd have to. They took the captain."

"Who did?" Lizzie quickly asked.

"The pirates," said the man. "The ones who brought us here."

Charlie piped up, "Is everyone alright? Did they hurt any of you?"

"Oh, no," said the co-pilot with the crowd of thousands looking on and listening in complete silence. "Only the ship. They disabled seven of our eight engines, and our radio. Don't think they wanted us leaving here anytime soon. And they robbed everyone on the ship of all money and jewelry. Oh, and they took three passengers with them, as well."

Charlie and Lizzie's hearts sunk as their eyes scanned the multitude forming behind the man with the white hat. They looked for two familiar faces in the crowd. They knew with close to ten thousand people on the ship, the likelihood of their parents being the passengers taken were not good, but still they had to ask.

"Three besides the captain? Who were they? And why would they TAKE them?" Charlie asked anxiously.

"Not sure of their names. One guy was a chemist, I believe, and the other two were a married couple... both were dentists."

Charlie and Lizzie's hearts sunk into their bellies with those words, and their faces turned pale.

"Are you sure?" Charlie demanded.

"For certain. I remember, because the leader of the group made a comment that 'two dentists were better than one', and that 'Goldtooth was going to be pleased with their find'." Many in the crowd behind him nodded in agreement.

"Goldtooth? Did you say Goldtooth?" asked the professor with great intrigue.

"That's right. I didn't quite understand it at the time, but now I'm thinking these pirates might be working for this 'Goldtooth' guy."

"Indeed," replied Professor Hootie, and you could almost see the cogs in his brain churning as if he were flipping through files to find the correct information.

"You know this guy, Professor?" asked Charlie.

"I know OF him," came the reply.

CHAPTER 8

GOLDTOOTH

"Professor Vardiman Goldstein was a professor at the University of the Milky Way long before I got there. In fact, he was one of the founders of the University and on the very first staff assembled," Professor Hootie began. "Professor Goldstein was a Fronkite which as you likely know have only two large square front teeth and no upper lips so their teeth are always seen. Well, legend has it that when Dr. Goldstein was only 6 months old and HIS two teeth came in, one of them came in made of gold. Hence, the nickname,

Goldtooth. It was said to be an anomaly that the doctors could not explain."

"But that doesn't make sense," Dr. Fox chimed in, "not the tooth part, although that is pretty remarkable itself, but Fronkites have a life expectancy of around 80 years, and you're saying this guy was one of the founders of the University. That would make him close to 300 years old."

"My thoughts exactly," said Professor Hootie. "But another interesting tidbit is that Professor Goldstein, or Goldtooth, was rumored to be part of the T.U.S.K., and by my estimations, he would likely have been one of the very last members."

"This is all too weird," said Lizzie. "So any idea on what he would want with our parents?"

The professor and Addison thought for a second and then he said, "This I cannot say, but it sounds like them being dentists is a factor."

Addison interrupted, "Just not sure what a man with only two teeth needs with a dentist… or a chemist… let's not forget that."

"So what's next?" asked Charlie, trying not to panic. "How do we find this guy that may, or may not be the real Goldtooth, and his band of pirates?"

"I think our best chance to find a clue is to try to find the secret lair of the T.U.S.K.," replied Dr. Hootie, "which if you recall, I believe to be on this very planet."

"So let's do that," Lizzie quickly agreed.

The professor once more addressed the man in the white hat, "Have you all encountered the local tribe on this island?" and he pointed to the island closest to the ship.

"Yes," said the man, "they have been cordial, but they are a bit aboriginal. No help with fixing the ship. A simple folk. Seems to be a very underdeveloped planet." The man paused, and then started back, "By the way, do you guys have any idea where we are?"

The professor turned to Charlie and nodded, "Elenarrus," Charlie told the man.

The man looked as if he'd never heard of it.

"Galaxy 6, System 1," stated Benny very matter of factly, proud he now knew something that someone else did not.

The man was startled that the hovering bug had spoken at all, but then said, "So we actually jumped galaxies. Wow. Well, thanks. That 'thing' we went through knocked out all our guidance and navigation systems."

"Those are called puddles," Benny said smugly like he'd known about puddles his whole life instead of having just learned about them in the last thirty minutes. Professor Hootie, Dr. Fox, Charlie, and Lizzie all found this humorous and giggled a bit.

Then Charlie, who was wearing one of Jagger's wristbands, touched the screen and said, "We're gonna need bikes."

They looked up at the Lady Alabama hovering nearby, and saw Jagger give a thumbs up through the windshield. The door on the side compartment of the craft opened and the flying motorbikes appeared and auto-piloted to the deck of the ship. Lizzie mounted the first bike, and Charlie the second, with Addison climbing on the back of his. They took off from the huge cruise ship heading for the closest island with the professor and Benny flying along beside them. Before they had gone too far, Charlie turned back and yelled to the crowd on the deck, "We will send help!"

And they were off.

CHAPTER 9

THE NATIVES

They found a clearing on a beach to land Lady Alabama and stash the bikes. As usual, Marvin hung back with the ship, just in case. Jagger grabbed himself a bag of Cheetos to have as a snack for the walk. As they started down a path into and through a lush tropical forest, Professor Hootie began to inform the rest of the crew about the natives of Elenarrus.

"The people here are called the Okapi*. It'll make sense when you see them. As the man said at the boat, they are a simple folk. Each island has a separate tribe. The tribes are friendly, but very competitive with each other."

"Can you speak their language?" asked Charlie.

"Actually, they speak English, but a 'more simple' form of it."

Just then, they rounded a corner in the path to see a wall of natives standing twenty yards ahead. Immediately the crew knew why they were referred to as the Okapi. These creatures had the torso and head of a deer with oversized ears and dark redish-brown fur. Each of the Okapi had a painted red stripe extending down the middle of their head to their nose. They had two legs, which were striped like a zebra's. The Okapi stood upright and walked like humans. Around their waists, they wore grass skirts made out of palm leaves. Their zebra striped arms ended with three fingered hands… hands that held spears.

The spears made the crew (other than Benny and Lizzie) a bit uncomfortable since only a few short days ago they had been on Trikre, where they had the Wermuth's spears pointed at their throats.

"You with others on big boat?" the Okapi in front asked.

"Sort of," said the professor. "We would like to help them, but need you to help us first."

"What we do to help?" asked the Okapi.

"We are looking for the place where the T.U.S.K. once met," said the professor.

All the Okapi gasped with the mention of the T.U.S.K. The leader Okapi replied, "These things we no discuss. These ghost stories from past. These forbidden islands."

"Forbidden islands?" Charlie asked with excitement realizing this was a lead. "Where are these 'forbidden islands'?"

"You need map. We no have map. Tribe Johnstoni have map. You want, we must win map."

"We want," said Jagger in his best Okapi voice, "How we win map?"

"We plan game. You follow." And with that the Okapi turned and led them further into the jungle until they reached a village of tall teepees.

The leader Okapi, whose name they learned was Greco, grabbed a short, curved horn and began to blow. He gave many blows, some long, some short, like he was doing Morse Code*. Within minutes, a reply came in from the distance in the form of another series of horn toots.

"It is set. Tribe Johnstoni come to us. Bring map. You win, get map. You lose, no map. They get," and he pointed in Jagger's direction. Everyone's eyes followed.

Jagger looked and realized what the Okapi was pointing at, "Ahh dude," he said, "not my Cheetos."

Charlie shrugged at him. Jagger shook his head and said, "Well… if I have to… and I guess we're not planning to lose whatever this is we are doing anyway, right?" He handed his bag over to the Okapi for safe keeping. Jagger then turned to Addison and whispered, "Anyway, I've got like ten more bags on the ship."

It took around an hour for Tribe Johnstoni to arrive. They looked almost exactly like the Okapi the crew had been interacting with, which they had now learned was called Tribe Artio. The only difference in their appearance was that Tribe Johnstoni had a blue stripe painted down their heads.

They all then went to a field that was in the middle of the island, where a sort of primitive obstacle course had been set up. Encircling the field, located in the surrounding trees, was a wooden bridge that was used by the spectators to look down onto the arena.

One Okapi climbed a ladder to a platform set high in a tree at the far end of the field. At the top, he revealed the map, and the onlookers clapped. Next he presented the bag of Cheetos, which captured an even bigger applause. He then shouted from the platform, "Choose two! First grab prize, win prize!"

Immediately two Okapi from Tribe Johnstoni stepped forward, and their tribe applauded the two competitors.

Greco, the leader of Tribe Artio, turned to the crew and spoke, "Challenge of two. They go with Koonga and Marku. Koonga and Marku fast. Koonga and Marku strong. My best not good as Koonga and Marku, but we try."

"Wait," started Charlie, "what do you mean 'YOU try?' Don't we get to choose who will race for us?"

"Yeah," Benny chimed in, "I guarantee I can get up there before they can."

"Flying no allowed. Run, jump, climb only. No fly," explained Greco.

"That's fine," Charlie said, "but I want to compete."

Jagger piped up in a macho tone, "Yeah, and I will, too."

"Sorry, Jagger," Charlie said. "No offense, but I want Lizzie as my partner."

"You sure, Chuck?, Jagger looked a bit stunned. "I know I'm not in peak condition, but I still move around pretty good."

"Trust me on this," Charlie replied in all seriousness. And at that moment, Jagger did trust him.

"Settled," said Greco, "boy compete, girl compete. That two." One of the other Okapi handed him a bucket. Greco dipped one of his three fingers into the bucket, pulled it out, and painted a red stripe down Charlie's head. He then did the same with Lizzie.

CHAPTER 10

THE COURSE

Lizzie and Marku were taken half way down the course, while Charlie and Koonga were led to the starting line. The Okapi stood close to seven feet tall and their muscles were extremely defined, but even more so on these two particular creatures.

Once in position, the competitors could see all the Okapi from the two tribes who had gathered on the wooden bridge in the trees. Then a voice announced through a megaphone of sorts, "These the rules! Many obstacle! You get past! Fast as can! However you can! No touch other runner! No touch water! You get prize first, you win prize!"

Charlie was a little intimidated by the seven foot tall beast standing next to him. He took a deep breath and gazed at the eighty meter sprint he had ahead of him, before the first obstacle.

The announcers voice came back through the megaphone, "You ready! You set! You…" he paused for dramatic effect, "GO!" Charlie and Koonga burst from their starting positions. Charlie ran like he'd never run before, and he was pretty fast… for an Earthling. But it was like racing a horse. Koonga's large muscular zebra legs churned at a pace Charlie couldn't keep up with, and the Okapi from Tribe Johnstoni took an early lead.

Koonga reached the first obstacle— two parallel logs, thirty feet long, lying across a water-filled trench. Charlie watched the Okapi quickly and gracefully scamper across one of the logs with his narrow hooves. Koonga jumped down from his log, just as Charlie was reaching his. But Charlie, having excellent balance, also swiftly ran across the log with out a hiccup.

At this point, he was about four seconds behind Koonga, who was now close to completing the next obstacle. This was an area thirty yards long which had numerous logs hanging above the course like a field of giant wind chimes. Charlie quickly realized that making it to this area of the course behind his competitor put him at an extreme disadvantage, because as Koonga passed through the relatively undisturbed field of hanging logs, he intentionally pushed and bumped as many as he could to set the whole field in motion. To Charlie, it was as if a strong breeze had blown in upon this land of wind chimes.

Charlie dodged and weaved through the logs. His reflexes from years of martial arts training serving him well... well almost. He was blindsided by a log and barely missed another as he was knocked to the ground. Lizzie cringed as her brother went down, losing even more time to Koonga— time that she knew SHE would have to try to make up.

"You've got this, B.B.!" she called out to her big brother.

Charlie went to the ground, but didn't dare stand right back up, for fear of getting cracked in the head with another swinging log. He rolled onto his back so that he could watch and time the logs. When the timing was right he leapt back to his feet and hastily weaved through the rest of the field unscathed.

Once out, he ran another fifty meters and was happy to see that Koonga had not gotten too far of a lead. Charlie was afraid he had fallen further behind after his mishap among the wind chimes. But the large Okapi, with the blue stripe down his face, was grabbing onto a vine at the next obstacle. As he ran, Charlie watched Koonga swing across another water-filled trench that was forty feet wide. When Charlie arrived at the edge of the trench, Koonga landed on the other side.

Charlie then spotted a target made of straw, with a second vine attached to it, across the water. He also found two piles of a fruit stacked in pyramid form. The fruit was similar to a smooth coconut, but about the size of baseball. He looked at the pile nearest the vine Koonga had swung across and quickly assessed that it had taken him five throws before he hit the target. Charlie knew this was where he could make up some ground on the half-deer, half-zebra creature. He grabbed the ball-like fruit that was at the apex of his pyramid, went into a baseball pitcher's wind-up, and hurled it at the bullseye forty feet away. The round fruit hit dead center, and like a dunking booth chair releasing its occupant into water, this hit target released a vine that swung across the trench to where Charlie was standing.

A yell of "Atta boy, Chuck!" came from the crowd in that Texan/surfer accent that Charlie had gotten to know all too well. He grabbed the vine, and with a running start, jumped at the edge of the trench, quickly swinging across to the other side.

He landed smoothly and knew he had made up a few seconds on his competitor, who was almost to reach the top of the next obstacle— a steeply inclined wall of interwoven rigid vines that peaked at twenty feet high, and then declined at the same steep angle coming down the back side. As he headed for this unique wall, he watched as one of Koonga's hooves slipped through a crack in the woven wall. He appeared to be stuck for a second or two. Charlie began to climb as the Okapi still struggled with getting his leg free. Koonga quickly got loose, topped the wall, and began his descent on the other side.

Young Mr. Paige climbed with calculated speed and did not make one single misstep on his ascent or descent of the porous wall. A quick ten yard sprint and he tagged Lizzie's hand. She started her portion of the race with a three second deficit.

She tore out after Marku, the Okapi she was racing, and the first obstacle ahead of her was a series of eight hurdles. As she began to run toward the first hurdle, she saw Marku glance back at her and grin. He then slowed just a bit, and with ease and overconfidence, jumped over the fifth hurdle in the series. As he reached the sixth one he actually dove over it, did a tuck-and-roll, and popped back up to his feet. He stood, arms raised, and listened to the applause from his needless, showy stunt. As he did, he looked back and spotted Lizzie in full stride hurdling the second hurdle like she was an Olympian. Never faltering, she continued her fast pace in his direction. He quickly realized she was making up ground faster than he imagined. His overconfidence was transformed into focus, and he turned to run once more.

Lizzie galloped over the remaining hurdles and started to the next obstacle. She came to her first water-filled trench. This one was the longest of the entire course. At the beginning of the trench, there were tree stumps cut at different heights, from quite low to quite high. Each stump was roughly a foot in diameter and there was a good four feet between each of them. She would have to find a path that led upward, because the second part of the obstacle, still over the small pond, was a multitude of vines, hanging from what appeared to be a giant willow tree*. The vines, closest to the stumps, had been trimmed, so that it took climbing the stumps like stairs to reach them. But this was easier said than done.

Marku was finding his way up the stumps and was nearing a stump tall enough for him to reach his first vine. Lizzie leapt from the edge of the trench onto the first stump, which was only inches higher than where she had jumped from. She landed cleanly on the stump and balanced herself. Looking down, she saw only water. She jumped to another stump with relative ease, then another, and then another. With her balance, she was making it look easy, climbing higher with each stump. She saw Marku now on the vines swinging from one to the other. He was almost halfway through them, when she found herself on a stump which had no stump near it that was a proper

height for jumping to. She had to make a deci
should she backtrack down some stumps to
the better path up, or should she try to some
get to the stump that was seven feet away from
and two feet higher than the one she was curre
on? She felt she had no choice. Backtrack
would take too long, so she rocked back sligh
and with all her might, she leapt with her arr
reached out for the higher stump. She did not go
far as she had hoped, but her finger tips reache
the edge of the sawed-off tree, and her bod
collided with the side of it. There was a collectiv
gasp from the onlookers.

Gripping the edges of the stump with onl
her fingers (up to the middle knuckle), and he
body dangling down the length of the tree, she
began to pull herself up. She grabbed the sides o
the stump with her feet, and pushed upward.
Quickly, she was able to get her forearms on top of

the sawed off tree. From there, she was able to pull the rest of her body onto the small platform. The audience began to applaud, and many, if not all, of them begin to chant, "Liz-zie, Liz-zie, Liz-zie."

This stump was high enough for her to reach the vines of the giant willow tree. She grabbed her first vine. Then, as if the vines were her dance partners, she smoothly, methodically, and very rapidly moved through them, one after the other until she was once again above solid ground.

Lizzie rushed to the next area which had two inclined narrow poles eight feet apart and leaning at a thirty-five degree angle to the ground. These led to an oversized set of monkey bars, that were twenty-five feet off the ground, and whose rungs were spread six feet apart. There were straight poles at the end of the monkey bars which allowed the competitors to safely slide down to the ground. THEN, just on the other side of this obstacle, Lizzie

could see "the finish line". After sliding down the pole from the high monkey bars, she would have to run ten yards and climb a vine forty feet straight up to the platform in the tree where the two potential prizes had been placed.

As Lizzie ran to this obstacle, she saw Marku make his way up the narrow inclined pole and reach for the first rung of the monkey bars. She had made up a little time on him in the vines, as her light, 100 pound, body was much speedier at transitioning from one vine to the next. But, she was still a good 8-10 seconds behind him, with not much course to go.

She ran to the underside of the inclined narrow pole and jumped to grab onto it at the highest point she could. She then threw her feet over the top of it and began to quickly shimmy up the pole. Again, she did this much faster than Marku. By the time she was reaching for the first rung of the large set of monkey bars, Marku had reached the last. Lizzie gripped the rung with one hand and swung, reaching her free hand out, and was just barely able to grab the next rung. She continued along so fluidly, once again much faster than the 280 pound Okapi.

However, at this point, Marku was already starting his ascent up one of the two tall vines toward the prize platform. He could almost taste those Cheetos.

Lizzie reached the final rung, and as everyone expected her to then slide down the pole, she didn't. The onlookers stood watching in confusion as the fifteen year old girl just hung there dangling twenty-five feet off the ground, with both hands gripping onto that last rung.

"What's she doing?" the professor whispered to the rest of the crew.

"I'm not sure," replied Dr. Fox.

"I'll tell you what she's doing," started Jagger, "she's letting that Okapi get further ahead. I knew I should have been Charlie's partner."

Just as he finished, they saw Lizzie take a big sigh, and she began to sway back and forth. She began pumping her legs and building up momentum.

"What is she doing?" Professor Hootie, Addison, Jagger, and Benny all asked again in unison. They diverted their gaze for only a moment to look at Charlie, still down in the arena. Like everyone else, he too, was watching his sister, and they spotted a faint smile form on his face. They quickly returned their eyes to Lizzie.

Lizzie began to bend at the waist, and keeping her legs tight together she flipped over the bar once. Then again. The third time she actually spread her legs into a split as she went over. Each time building speed as she rotated around that final rung.

The audience continued to watch in wonder. For a second time in only minutes, this young girl looked like some sort of Olympic athlete. Even Marku, who was a third of the way up his vine, paused to see what young Miss Paige was up to. After the fifth rotation around, and just barely missing hitting her toes on the rung before the last one, she had built up considerable speed and she released from the bar. She went flying... flipping once in the air, and headed right for the vines which hung from the prize platform. And to everyone's awe, she not only made the distance, but she was also able to grab onto her vine without falling, and she did so HALF WAY up the vine.

"I thought they said 'no flying'," Jagger commented to Benny with a smile.

Marku looked UP at his competitor, who was now in the lead. Lizzie gave a quick grin to him, and in an instant began climbing the vine. No matter how fast the large Okapi with the blue stripe tried to climb, it was no match for the climbing speed of the lightweight, red-striped, Lizzie Paige.

Lizzie reached the top, pulled herself onto the platform, grabbed the map, and raised it over her head. Both tribes, the crew, and Charlie all burst into applause.

Marku finished climbing and met Lizzie on the platform only twelve seconds later. He was out of breath and looked defeated. Lizzie reached down, grabbed the bag of Cheetos, opened it, and offered them to her opponent.

CHAPTER 11

THE MAP

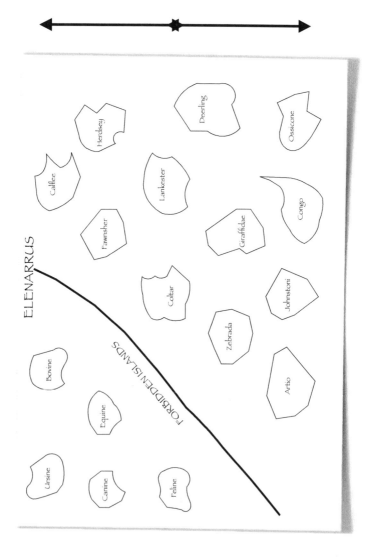

(Which island do YOU think they should go to?)

The crew of the Lady Alabama took a picture of the map of Elenarrus, and left the original with Tribe Artio. They went back to their ship, where Marvin converted the map into a large hologram in the center of the cabin. They studied the map. It consisted of two different groupings of islands. The first grouping was twelve islands of almost identical size. This group of islands was named for the tribes that lived on them, or perhaps the other way around, but nonetheless, Charlie and Lizzie and the rest of the crew saw the island names of Artio, Johnstoni, Congo, Zebrada, Giraffidae, Ossicone, etc…

Then there was the second grouping of islands. These were a bit smaller and further west than the other islands. Near this grouping on the map, written in all capital letters were the words "FORBIDDEN ISLANDS".

Jagger pointed to these islands on the map, "Pretty sure these are the ones we're looking for."

The professor rolled his eyes and said, "Nice detective work, Captain Obvious."

They read the names of the "Forbidden Islands" which all seemed to have a commonality. They all ended in the same three letters… -ine.
There was Feline, Canine, Equine, Bovine, and Ursine.

"They're all animals," Lizzie stated.

"She's right," Dr. Fox confirmed.

"So which of these animals has a tusk?" Benny asked. "I'm guessing that's what we are looking for here."

"You may be right," said Professor Hootie. "Let's see now… well, Feline is a cat."

"And Canine is a dog," stated Lizzie.

"Pretty sure Equine means horse," said Charlie. "Can't think of what Ursine is, though."

Jagger chimed in, "Is that like Ursa Major* and Ursa Minor*?"

"Oh yeah," said Charlie, "the constellations... Great Bear and Little Bear. So Ursine must refer to a bear."

"Excellent work," stated the professor. "How about the last one? Bovine? Anyone know that one?"

"It's a cow," stated Dr. Fox. "We use bovine bone sometimes when we have to do bone grafts on patients at the hospital. The graft material is taken from the hind leg of cows, and is called bovine bone."

"Very well, then. I believe we have all five... cats, dogs, horses, bears, and cows," stated the professor.

"So which one has a tusk?" asked Benny, obviously not familiar with the animals listed.

"Well," stated Addison, "none of them really."

"What about a saber-toothed tiger*?" asked Lizzie. "Tigers would be in the feline family."

They all thought for a bit. Then the professor said, "Well, I can't think of any dogs, bears, horses, or cows that have tusks, so maybe the saber-toothed tiger does point us to the island of Feline?"

"Maybe," said Addison, "but I'm just not sure that the saber-toothed tiger was really considered to have tusks, but more just overgrown teeth. That's why they called them 'saber-toothed' instead of 'saber-tusked'."

"Yeah," started Charlie, "but what are tusks really? Just overgrown canines. Right?"

"Say what?" asked Jagger. "Canines?"

"Yeah, canines. You do remember that our parents are dentists? We've picked up the lingo through the years. Canines are what you call the pointy corner teeth," Charlie stated as he touched his upper left canine with his index finger.

"That's right," confirmed Dr. Fox, like a light bulb had just gone off in her head. "And he is right... all tusks ARE just overgrown canine teeth." She grinned, "They were trying to trick us."

"They led us to think 'Canine' referred to a dog," said Professor Hootie having caught on to Addison's light-bulb moment, "but in fact, it is just a synonym of tusk." He turned to Jagger, "Captain, I think you should take us to Canine."

"Roger that," replied Jagger, and Marvin put his hand to his forehead and saluted. Jagger then said to him, "Little buddy, I think those guys," and he pointed toward the cruise ship that was anchored off shore from them, "need you a little more than us right now."

Marvin sunk a little in disappointment, but then nodded in agreement.

They flew once again above the deck of the Saint Louis the Lionhearted, and Marvin with a toolbox in hand was dropped to the deck. As they took off they saw him give a big thumbs up to the Lady.

Chapter 12

The Forbidden Island

Jagger did a quick fly-by of the small island, but nothing could be seen from the air, except a canopy of thick vegetation. The captain landed the ship on a beach, and the crew walked out into the sand.

"You sure this is the one?" Jagger asked, directed at Professor Hootie.

"I feel certain," replied Dr. Fox.

"So what's the plan," asked Lizzie.

Benny chimed in, "I'll scout it. Wait right here." The smallest of the crew then took off, flying at a velocity that the others were still in awe of. He weaved through the thick vegetation with ease and speed.

Professor Hootie stated, "I knew those little guys could fly super fast through space within their own system, but I did not know they were capable of that type of speed otherwise."

"Yeah," said Charlie, "the queen indicated he had a 'special talent'. I don't think Benny's speed is a common thing for all Muzz Bugs."

About ten minutes passed and the navy and gold speedster emerged from the jungle. "Well, I didn't see much, but I did find some statues about two miles deep. Nothing else that caught my eye really."

"Statues? Of what?" asked Charlie.

"Looked like some animals. Maybe four of them. Not sure though. They were covered with a lot of ivy and I was moving pretty fast," replied Benny.

"Sounds like something we should definitely check out," Dr. Hootie stated.

The others agreed. So they hiked through the thick jungle carrying laser machetes to help them clear paths to walk. Sure enough almost two miles in, they spotted the first statue. They came up from behind it, and they could tell from the tail that it was a large stone scorpion* on the pedestal. There was ivy and other vegetation growing on and around it.

As they reached the statue, they saw three others obscured by the overgrown jungle. It was obvious no one had been here for a very long time.

"Let's clear the area out," requested Charlie. They fanned out, and wielding their laser machetes, cleared away the vegetation around the statues. This took a few minutes, but once they were done, they could see each of the statues clearly. The four statues which were fifteen feet from the other. Each facing one of the other statues. The scorpion was facing a stone kangaroo, and there was a tiger facing a unicorn.

The crew examined the animals, and one thing quickly caught their attention. The tiger's mouth was open like it was growling, trying to scare away an intruder. It had vicious, sharp teeth. This was NOT what they found odd. They looked at the scorpion's face, and it too, had just as vicious of a scowl, and just as sharp of teeth. Then they looked at the unicorn (once thought to be mystical and most often thought of as peaceful) with big, sharp teeth that seemed to tell the tiger it was facing that it was not afraid of the massive feline.

Then there was the kangaroo. "That's one mean marsupial!" Jagger commented, because it, too, had a face to fear. It was like the tiger's mouth had been superimposed onto these other animals, and the crew found it strangely disturbing.

They all went from statue to statue looking for markings, or words, or some sort of clue as to what they should do next and to where this "secret lair of the T.U.S.K" was. Lizzie climbed up on the pedestal with the unicorn and looked it directly in the face and said, "None of the carousels I ever rode had these," and she put her finger on the sharp tip of the unicorn's lower left canine... and it moved.

The tooth was on a hinge and it bent forward when she applied pressure. It startled her at first, and she quickly jerked her hand back as if the creature might come alive and bite her. But when nothing happened, she pulled the tooth again, and yelled out, "Hey guys, look at this! I think I found something!"

The other five crew members quickly assembled around Lizzie and the ferocious unicorn, and watched as she demonstrated the moving, hinged tooth.

"That's great," said Charlie, "but what does it do?"

"I don't know," replied Lizzie, "but it's something."

Addison had slipped over to the scorpion statue and she called out, "This one has it, too!" She moved aside so they could see from where they were standing, and she gave it a tug. But, just like with the unicorn, nothing seemed to happen.

Charlie ran to the tiger statue and Jagger to the kangaroo, and both confirmed that these statues had the same movable canine.

"Maybe they're broken," stated Jagger, "I mean this place does look pretty forgotten about."

"No, no," said Professor Hootie clearly contemplating the situation. "Maybe, just maybe," he began to have another one of those lightbulb moments, "maybe there is a combination."

"What do you mean, doc," asked Jagger, "like scorpion, kangaroo, tiger, unicorn? Or something like that?"

"Yes, or something like that," said the professor.

(Can YOU figure out the correct combination?)

They all paused and thought for a bit. Then, after only about a minute Lizzie called out, "Charlie, you go first! Pull the tiger tooth, then I'll pull, then Addison, and then Jagger! I figured it out!"

The others obviously had not yet figured it out, but they followed her orders nonetheless, each pulling on the lower left canine tooth of their statue in the exact sequence that Lizzie had called out. Then when Jagger had bent the fourth tooth, the kangaroo tooth, something began to happen. It was like a small earthquake was occurring, and they began to see ivy being ripped from the side of a hill close by, as a wall of the mountain opened and slid, and a doorway into the side of the hill was exposed.

After the astonishment of the hidden door faded, they all looked back at Lizzie, and the professor started to ask, "How... why did you...?"

Lizzie interrupted him, "T...U...S...K. Tiger...Unicorn...Scorpion...Kangaroo," she said simply and matter of factly.

The professor grinned and said, "Of course, you clever girl. Of course."

CHAPTER 13

THE SECRET LAIR

They entered the open door in the side of the hill. It felt like they were entering a tomb. It was dark and musty at the entrance. They used the light from their laser machetes to help them see. Thirty feet in, the cave bent to the left, and as soon as they made the turn, they found themselves at a large metal door. Charlie reached for the handle and pulled back on it. A puff of steam released from around the door, but it opened with ease as Charlie pulled on it.

Much to their surprise, as it opened, lights began to light up along the corridor ahead of them, like the lights in a movie theater's aisle. Then a bright light came on down the way, as if an entire room had lit up. They quickly made their way down the lit path, and found themselves inside the secret lair of the T.U.S.K.

It was a large, circular room that did not look ancient at all. It was sleek, clean, and modern in every way. Compared to the rest of Elenarrus, it was very much out of place. Charlie couldn't help but think that it was like a little slice of Nucleus had been placed on Elenarrus.

Half of the circular room was lined with book shelves, filled with books that for the most part all looked the same. They were of different thicknesses, but all white covers with hand written titles in black down their spines. The other half of the room was a large curved video monitor. Charlie leaned in to Lizzie and joked, "Look, it's a super cool, top secret iMax theater."

In the middle of the room was a large circular table, with a hole in the middle of it. It was surrounded by twenty chairs. Jagger sat in one, and pushed a button on one of the arms. The chair began to vibrate and give him a back massage.

"Addy," he said with his voice shaking with the vibrations, yet completely relaxed, "you have GOT to try this."

Addison, Charlie, and Lizzie grabbed a chair and decided to try it out. Addison pushed a button on the left arm of her chair, and when she did, the lights dimmed slightly and a hologram of a lady appeared out of the hole in the center of the table. She was not a human lady, but had a wide, light pink face with dark blue eyes, and three hot pink feathery protrusions extending from each side of her head that seemed to be blowing in a strong breeze. She wore a large silver robe with a hood that was off her head, and on the left chest area of the robe in black letters was the word "QASSI".

"Welcome, worthy members of the T.U.S.K. My name is Qassi," which she pronounced like Cassie. "What may I assist you with today?" came the very pleasant and calm female voice.

"She's a Fimp," said Dr. Fox.

"From the planet BitBit, no doubt," stated Professor Hootie.

"She's an A.I.," stated Jagger matter of factly. "Artificial Intelligence all the way."

"I agree," replied Addison, "but obviously modeled after a Fimp. Look at her resemblance to an axolotl*. That's Alien Anatomy 101 right there," she said and winked in the direction of Charlie and Lizzie.

The crew thought a second before answering, and Charlie then asked, "Are there any secrets dealing with teeth and chemistry?" The rest of the crew nodded in affirmation that this was a good question, considering they had been told two dentists and a chemist had been taken from the cruise ship.

Qassi's deep blue eyes began to flicker, as she processed the question. Then, the flickering stopped. "In our library, we have 1,428 references to chemistry," the calm, soothing voice of Qassi answered, "and 132 references to teeth."

The crew sighed with discouragement, "It'll take forever sifting through all those," commented Benny.

"They sure do have a lot of secrets around here," followed Jagger.

"But," continued Qassi, the word causing the crew to move to the edge of their seats in anticipation of her next words, "cross-referencing the two, I find that there are only 3 books which deal with both 'chemistry' and 'teeth'. The first is titled, <u>Molar Energy</u>, the second titled, <u>The Power of Baby Teeth</u>, and the third titled, <u>Teeth Whitening for Any Species</u>."

The six of them jumped from their seats and went running to the book shelves along the opposite wall to find what seemed like an ocean of books. The shelves went from floor to ceiling, and it was a tall ceiling. There were twenty rows of shelves that curved around the wall for two hundred feet. They were quickly relieved to find that the books were organized in alphabetical order by title. They hurriedly looked for the three books.

"Up here," called out Benny near the next to top shelf, "I found the 'Baby Tooth' one."

Lizzie climbed a ladder which was connected to the shelves by wheels. Charlie pushed his sister on the ladder, around the arc, to where Benny the Muzz Bug had called out. Benny did not have the capabilities of removing and carrying the book from the shelf himself, so Lizzie did the honors and removed the first of the books.

"Found Molar Energy," exclaimed Addison only seconds later, retrieving another of the white faced books with black writing from a shelf about chest high.

Then, only about a minute more passed before they saw Professor Hootie fly fifteen rows up and remove another book, announcing, "And I have the 'whitening' one."

They reconvened at the large circular table and laid the three books out and began to read them to see if they could determine which of these books might give them clues about where to find the Paiges.

The professor skimmed through the whitening book, and Addison the one titled Molar Energy with Jagger peering over her shoulder.

Charlie and Lizzie flipped through <u>The Power of Baby Teeth</u>.

After several minutes of reading, the professor spoke up first, "I cannot imagine a scenario where anyone would kidnap people to create the substance known as 'Dentablanca' out of 'sodium hydroxide' and 'gloxmorolol', which according to this can only be extracted from the oceans of the planets Savett and Jimjub. Seems like a lot of trouble to go through to brighten some smiles."

"Well," Addison started, "this one describes how molars of more that 2,000 species of creatures can actually be used as batteries when infused with a substance known as 'plutoaranium'. It says that 'four molars can put out enough energy to power a vehicle'. What do you think?" Dr. Fox looked over at her former teacher.

"Hmm, maybe. How about you guys? Is <u>The Power of Baby Teeth</u> about using baby teeth as batteries, as well?" Professor Hootie asked Charlie and Lizzie who were still engrossed in reading their book and had not even listened to what the others were saying. "Charlie-boy," the professor said a little louder trying to get his attention.

"Huh?" he perked up. "What was that?"

"Your book... anything good?"

"Fascinating," Lizzie remarked without pulling her eyes from the pages.

"Well, tell us," insisted the professor, becoming impatiently curious. "What is 'the power of baby teeth'?"

Lizzie finally pulled from her trance-like reading, looked up at the rest of the crew and stated, "Eternal youth."

Chapter 14

The Power of Baby Teeth

"Ding ding ding! We have a winner!" exclaimed Jagger.

The others closed the books in front of them and crowded around Lizzie and Charlie.

"What do you mean 'eternal youth'?" asked Professor Hootie. "How is that possible?"

"Well," Lizzie began, "this says that baby tooth dust, which is just baby teeth ground into a fine powder, have to be mixed with three other substances. It gives very specific detailed amounts of each. Look," she turned back three pages, "it's like a recipe."

They all looked on and read the words: "Add 1 kilogram of baby tooth dust, plus 35.7 milliliters of flotonium bisulbate, plus 18.5 milliliters of cragnomagflesium, plus 2 milligrams of purple moon rock powder into container and mix thoroughly. Heat over flame until frothy. Let cool for 5 minutes, and then chug."

"Doesn't seem like they'd need dentists to tell them what's a baby tooth," said Jagger.

"Well," Lizzie began, and she flipped two pages ahead, "there is this." She pointed to the middle of one of the pages.

It read, "WARNING: There must be no decay on any of the baby teeth used. If any decay is present, then the reverse effect will occur and instead of remaining youthful, your body will begin to decay and get old at an extremely rapid rate."

"So all the teeth have to be examined thoroughly and if any cavities are seen they must be thrown out," Charlie explained. "This has to be where our parents come into the picture."

"Indeed," said Professor Hootie, "indeed." The others could almost see the wheels in his head spinning again, trying to process all the information.

"And," added Dr. Fox, "I guess we've solved the riddle of how Dr. Vardiman Goldstein, a.k.a. Goldtooth, could still be alive."

"So does the book say where to go?" asked Benny.

"I'm assuming to a planet with a purple moon," replied Jagger.

"No," stated the professor, quickly negating Jagger's assumption. "The recipe only calls for 2 milligrams of purple moon rock dust. That is a tiny amount. You could break off a good chunk of rock and have plenty for years. There would be no need in living near a purple moon. But, one KILOGRAM of baby tooth dust... that's A LOT of baby teeth."

"You're right," Lizzie confirmed. "The book estimates 300 baby teeth ground up to equal one kilogram. And that's needed every day."

"Where in the world would anyone find that many baby teeth?" asked Addison.

"Well, that's what we intend to figure out, my dear, because I have a feeling if we find the baby teeth, we find their parents," stated Professor Hootie.

Lizzie flipped through the remainder of the book quickly and felt confident in stating, "There is no mention of how to locate any of the substances used, including the teeth."

The professor looked up to the center of the table where the axolotl-like lady was still hovering and he asked, "Qassi, where can an abundance of baby teeth be found?"

Her eyes flickered briefly, and Qassi replied, "I can only find one reference to the location of an abundance of baby teeth. It is titled, <u>A Multitude of Deciduous Teeth</u>."

"Wait," said Jagger, "what are deciduous teeth?"

"Just another name for baby teeth," Charlie answered.

"They can also be called 'primary' teeth," Lizzie chimed in. "We told you we've picked up on the lingo," she smiled and gave Jagger a wink.

The crew quickly returned to the large book case along the back wall.

"The M's were in this area," called out Addison, who had found the book titled <u>Molar Energy</u> moments ago, and had gone straight back to that spot. She hastily skimmed the titles on the spines, but slowed as she got closer and read, "<u>Multiple Personality Planets</u>… <u>Mummy Mysteries</u>

Solved... wait." She reread the spines, she looked ahead a few books, and then she announced, "It's not here!"

"What?" Charlie asked desperately. "Let me see." He eased around to where Addison was standing and also read the spines. "She's right," he confirmed, "and this one, <u>Mummy Mysteries Solved</u>, is actually leaning a bit, like another book is supposed to be here." Addison hadn't noticed it before, but now she saw that he was correct in his observation.

They returned to the table and Benny asked, "So what do we do?"

Lizzie spoke up, "Qassi, that book is missing from the library, do you have any backup files on the book <u>A Multitude of Deciduous Teeth</u>?"

"I will check on that for you," came Qassi's calm voice and her eyes began to flicker. This time it took a little longer than the previous times, but finally she replied, "These files have been deleted from my system."

Charlie spoke up, "Qassi, please try to do a retrieval of deleted files titled <u>A Multitude of Deciduous Teeth</u>."

"I will see what I can do," Qassi replied. This time her eyes closed slowly. Then, they reopened quickly, but instead of flickering light, her eyes were filled with crackling snow, as if the cable had gone out on a television. Little white and black lights popping over the entirety of her eyes. This went on for longer than any of the previous flickering had, but finally her eyes closed. And when they reopened, they were again blue.

"I could not retrieve the text from this book," she stated. "However, I was able to retrieve these three images." At that moment three images appeared onto the large curved screen in front of them.

U	X	H	J	R	C	O	F
B	E	A	M	O	R	P	K
F	U	L	L	M	E	U	T
G	L	F	I	V	S	F	I
Y	N	E	G	W	C	X	D
X	E	V	H	B	E	P	E
K	W	L	T	B	N	V	S
S	R	O	C	K	T	O	I

D	I	A	M	O	N	D	P
X	E	A	R	V	F	B	H
K	D	O	U	J	B	P	O
E	W	O	R	M	O	S	N
Y	W	B	K	C	X	N	E
K	W	E	D	D	I	N	G
S	V	L	L	G	N	A	V
G	O	L	D	E	G	J	A

(Turn this way)

123

The crew stared at the screen and the images. Two of them were grids of letters that appeared to be some sort of word searches, only without a key of words to find. The other appeared to be symbols— possibly letters to a foreign language.

(Can YOU help them solve the puzzles?)

"Professor," Charlie asked, "is that a language you know?"

"No," stated the professor. "I'm not even positive that it is a language… but maybe."

"There," shouted Lizzie and she pointed to the word search furtherest to the left, "I see the word DIAMOND. On the top line there."

"Yes. I see it too, dear," said the professor. "Very good, Lizzie, why don't you and Addison find as many words as you can in that grid, and Charlie, you and Jagger work on the other grid. Maybe they will form a sentence that will give us a clue."

"Like we did with the words we found on the squid," stated Jagger with a smile.

"Exactly," Professor Hootie responded. Benny and I will see what we can figure out about these symbols."

Everyone agreed to this, and they spent about ten minutes working on their respective puzzles.

(Did YOU work on the puzzles?)

"So these are the words we found," Addison spoke first. "DIAMOND, EAR, KEY, WORM, WEDDING, GOLD, BOXING, BELL, and PHONE."

Lizzie chimed in, "We feel very confident that this is not supposed to be a sentence, but a word that is a common theme between these words."

Professor Hootie appeared intrigued by the statement, but before he could even try to link the words together for himself, Lizzie blurted out in what seemed like only one breath, "And we are quite certain that word is RING. Bells and phones both ring, and then there's a diamond ring, a gold ring, a wedding ring, an earring, a key ring, a boxing ring, and ringworm…"

"Which isn't a worm at all, but instead a fungal infection of the skin, or scalp," interjected Addison.

Benny was visibly confused and a little grossed out, especially at Dr. Fox's interjection.

"Think I could have done with out that last part," he stated quietly.

Impressed, the professor said, "Well done, I couldn't agree with you ladies more." He paused, then said with a grin, "And how did the boys' team do?"

"Pretty good, we think," said Charlie. "We found the words FULL, SCENT, ROCK, BEAM, LIGHT, HALF, and NEW."

"I was trying to unscramble the sentence," started Jagger, "but now I'm thinking that's not gonna happen. And good thing, too, because I was not making any sense of a sentence with these words."

"Yeah," Charlie followed, "not positive what the common link is yet."

"It's MOON," exclaimed Lizzie confidently.

"Well, I thought of that," said Charlie, "but how does SCENT go with MOON? Is there some girly perfume I've never heard of called Moon-scent that you wear?" Charlie kidded his sister.

"No, B.B., but if you had solved the puzzle correctly you would see that you missed the word

'TIDES' on the far right side, and that SCENT is not SCENT at all— it is CRESCENT. So you have a new moon, full moon, CRESCENT moon," she really emphasized that one, "moon rock, moonbeam, moonlight, and moons control the tides." She took a breath and smirked at her brother.

"Boom!' shouted Benny. "You've been served! This girl is good!"

Charlie just rolled his eyes having realized Lizzie was right about it all, and everyone else laughed.

"How about you, Professor," asked Addison, "have you and Benny figured out the other image?"

"Actually, we have not," the professor stated disappointingly. "For a bit I thought maybe the second and third characters represented hills and valleys, and then again as the sixth and seventh characters, but now I'm convinced that they are indeed a language that I just can't seem to put my talon on."

"It's English," Charlie piped up enthusiastically, hoping to redeem himself.

Lizzie glared at him and said, "How do you figure that?"

"Yes, how indeed?" repeated the professor.

Charlie called out, "Qassi, could I get a print out of the third image, please?"

"I can accommodate that," replied Qassi.

A sheet of paper with the image of the symbols emerged from a little slit in a wall near by, which Charlie quickly retrieved. He looked around the room until he spotted what he was looking for. He went to a wall toward the bookshelves, as the others watched with curiosity of what exactly he was up to. Charlie pulled a small, square mirror off the wall. He brought it and the printed image back to the large table where the others were waiting.

He laid the mirror face up on the table, and then folded the piece of paper to where the crease was at the very bottom of the strange symbols, and then placed the paper on the mirror to where the crease touched the mirror. And like magic, the strange symbols were no longer strange. It was as easy as reading any other word written in English.

"Boxchox," read Charlie, as he glanced at Lizzie and gloated with a smug smile.

BOX CHOX

(Turn this way)

CHAPTER 15

THE MOON OF BOXCHOX

"**B**oxchox, that's a planet just one galaxy over in Galaxy 7, System 3, I believe," stated Jagger.

"I believe you are correct indeed," affirmed Professor Hootie.

"Well let's go!" exclaimed Lizzie. "It seems obvious that we need to go to Boxchox's moon."

"Except," started Jagger, "if I recall correctly, Boxchox has fifteen moons."

"We'll figure it out," said Lizzie, "but those people… those pirates have our parents, and it sounds like they are basically treating them like slaves. So, we need to go!"

The others agreed and they quickly began to leave the way they came in, down the lighted theater-like hallway. As they did, they heard Qassi say, "Thank you and have a nice day."

They hastily made their way back through the jungle, following the path they'd cleared with the laser machetes on their way in. They boarded the Lady Alabama and Jagger asked, "Hey Chuck, wanna be my co-pilot?"

Charlie excitedly replied, "You know it!" and he went to Marvin's seat, plopped down, and began to study the controls. He actually felt pretty confident with it all, as he had been watching and almost studying Jagger and Marvin over the last week of travels.

They quickly took to the sky and into hyper speed to travel to the next galaxy.

They slowed as they entered System 3 of Galaxy 7 so as to not overshoot Boxchox. This system had eight planets, all relatively close together, and all could be seen in a single view. Charlie noticed right away that this seemed like a very active system. They could see lots of other spaceships flying between planets. Lizzie spotted Boxchox immediately, due to the numerous moons surrounding the planet. Only one of the other planets had more than one moon, but it only had three. There were two planets that had no moon at all. Boxchox seemed to be a bit of an outlier planet, with not as much traffic around it.

"Um," started Jagger nervously, "I know it seems like it would be quicker to fly straight toward Boxchox, but I really think we should kind of go around these other planets," he paused and stuttered a bit, "you know stay out of possible traffic, and... well... and... the inhabitants of this system can be a bit... um... suspicious and nosey... so it would be better to just keep a low profile."

"I concur," stated the professor, "a bunch of questioning from the locals could take longer."

The others agreed and Jagger sighed with relief. So, he steered around the outskirts of the system and as they neared Boxchox, they were better able to view its fifteen moons.

"Bingo!" exclaimed Lizzie pointing to one of the planet's moons. The rest of the crew saw it a half second later and knew the teenager was right.

There were five white moons, three yellow moons, three orange moons, two blue moons, one pink moon, and one moon that was teal with a purple ring around it. This was the one Lizzie was pointing to.

"Boxchox, moon, ring. Told you we'd figure it out," she stated.

The Lady Alabama was flown to the surface of the teal moon with the ring around it. Due to the lack of atmosphere, Charlie, Lizzie, Addison, and Jagger put on space suits with helmets, which allowed them to breathe on the surface of the moon. Professor Hootie also needed a helmet, but no suit. And Benny needed nothing at all.

Like Earth's moon, this ringed moon of Boxchox had many craters and hills. The surface was like a soft dirt, but crunched with each step, as if gravel was mixed in with it.

Addison leaned down and scooped up a handful of the dirt. She made a fist, and shook her hand allowing the dirt to sift through the cracks in her gloved fingers. When she felt all the dirt was gone, she opened her fist and found four small, hard, white objects.

"Baby teeth," she muttered to herself. Then aloud she said, "Yep, we're definitely in the right place," and she held up a baby incisor to show the rest.

"Weird," said Charlie.

"Creepy," corrected Jagger.

They removed the flying motor bikes from the side compartments on the ship, and went to explore the moon for signs of life. Charlie drove one bike with Addison on the back, and Benny flew along side them in one direction. Jagger flew the other bike with Lizzie, and the professor flew with them in the other direction. This way they could stay in constant communication with each other via the bikes' radios.

Watching the surface of the moon pass below him as he flew, Charlie found it interestingly amusing that the color reminded him of toothpaste. But he also started to notice something else.

"Are you seeing this?" he asked Addison over his shoulder.

"Yes," she stated, "the concentration of baby teeth seems to be increasing."

Charlie radioed to Jagger's group, "Hey guys, I think you might want to come this direction. There's a lot more baby teeth where we are now."

"Roger that," replied Jagger, who was actually off his bike. He, Lizzie, and Professor Hootie had stopped. They were sifting some moon dirt, and not finding any teeth. "We'll head back your way."

Before the others could reach them though, Charlie, Addison, and Benny, basically following a path of baby teeth, flew down into a large crater. They came upon what looked like a little abandoned village. It was like no village they had ever seen before. Every house, every bench, every structure in the village was made out of baby teeth.

But they still found no signs of life. They climbed off their bike and walked around looking for clues of what happened to the inhabitants of this village.

Soon, the other three crew members made it to the village as well, and they joined the others in looking around.

"Can I just say again," started Jagger, "that this is creepy. All these little teeth… I mean… CREE-PEE!"

"I think it's cute," retorted Lizzie, "and amazing. Look at this place!" she said in a voice of wonder.

Then, they all heard Benny call out, "Over here!" and they all ran towards his voice.

When they reached him, he said, "I can't read, but I do know that those are words." He pointed to a sign on the door of one of the larger buildings in the village.

On a door made of baby teeth there was a wooden sign which seemed completely out of place in this village and on this moon. In large letters, with some form of ink, were written the words "WE HAVE MOVED".

The crew all read the words to themselves and stood there in complete disbelief. "You've got to be kidding me," said Lizzie, completely bummed by this finding. She, like the rest of them, knew this meant more time they would have to spend trying to figure out where the pirates took her parents. And she was not sure where they would now look. It seemed like this whole trip had lead them to a dead end. "Well," she said, "what now?"

"Back to Elenarrus, I suppose," stated the professor. "To the lair of the T.U.S.K."

"I suppose that is our best chance," stated Jagger. "Maybe Qassi can help us figure out where we should look next."

"Maybe," said Charlie, "but maybe there's another clue here. I mean, does it not seem strange to anyone else that there is a piece of wood on a moon with no trees? Maybe the wood came from where these people moved to."

"I have to admit," stated Dr. Fox, "I only took one botany class through my entire schooling, and I do not remember much. My focus was much more on anatomy."

At this point, Charlie had walked all the way up to the sign to study it. Running his gloved fingers along the edges, then looking closely at the grain of the wood. As he did, he noticed something and he called out, "Hey guys, I think I found something."

Lizzie rolled her eyes in disbelief, "B.B., when did you get to be an expert on wood."

"No," he said excitedly, "the line below the word 'HAVE'," he paused and turned back to face the group, "It's a sentence!"

Chapter 16

Deciphering the Tiny Clue

"It's really small, and very hard to read, but it's definitely a sentence," stated Charlie.

They all gathered with him at the sign and squinted their eyes trying to read it. It was difficult enough, but with their helmets on, it became nearly impossible for them to see clearly.

"Are you sure, Chuck? I can't make out a thing," remarked Jagger.

Benny chimed in, having the smallest set of eyes of the group, and no helmet, "Oh yeah, he's right. I can see it clear as day."

"Well what's it say?" asked Lizzie impatiently.

"Um...," started Benny, "maybe you didn't catch what I said earlier, but I can't read. There. You happy? You made me say it again. I'm not proud of it," he said sadly.

"Sorry," said Lizzie sincerely. "I forgot."

"I have an idea," said Jagger, then he slid his sleeve up, and exposed his wristband. He touched a few buttons and turned it toward the sign. He touched another button which took a picture. He then zoomed in on the tiny words and read, **"Where a meteor incised and one became two, a species does live and myth becomes true."**

(Do YOU know where they need to go?)

Charlie turned to Lizzie and said, "Now this sounds like something we would have heard while trying to save you." Addison, Professor Hootie, and Jagger all nodded.

"But what does it mean?" Lizzie insisted.

"Well," said the professor, "let's break it down."

"Do you think the word 'incised' is perhaps talking about teeth? Like incisors? We have been dealing with 'canines' a lot," Charlie said.

"Yes," answered the professor, "but that was from the T.U.S.K., and this clue is not… at least I don't think it is. I am thinking of 'incised' like a surgeon makes an incision with a scalpel. Except in the clue, it is a meteor that is the scalpel. That is the way I read it."

"I agree," stated Addison.

"So," Lizzie began, "for a meteor to cut it in half, instead of just crush it, we are talking about something big, like another moon or planet, right?"

"Indeed," replied the professor.

"So do you know of any planets or moons that are cut in half?" asked Charlie.

The professor shook his head.

"One thing that strikes me," said Dr. Fox, "is how it says 'one became two', not simply 'cut in half' or 'cut into two pieces'. It just keeps conjuring up images for me of a surgery I observed during my medical residency. I got to see a set of conjoined Kelf twins be surgically separated."

"Wait," said Jagger, "that's it."

"What's it?" asked Addison.

"What you just said... twins. Conjoined twins. 'One becomes two'. The twin planets. Castor and Pollux."

"Of course," said Professor Hootie digging deep into his brain's data bank. "It is believed that thousands of years ago those two planets were actually connected by a narrow land mass, until a meteor directly hit that area, and forever separated the planets. That is why they sit so close together. But to my knowledge, both planets are uninhabited , which is probably why I didn't think of it earlier. No languages, no relics, no cultures of any sort, not much of anything to teach about," the professor stated as an excuse for his oversight.

"Sounds like a perfect pirate hideout to me," stated Charlie.

"Well, I stopped on Castor when I was there fifteen years ago to reset Bella's navigational system, and just to get my feet on some ground. Remember, I had been in space for around three weeks. And you're right, doc, I didn't see a soul.

Seemed pretty barren. A bit of a cold wasteland, best I can recall."

"Okay," said Charlie, "maybe not the hideout I'd choose, but still sounds like that's our place."

"Indeed," stated the professor. "Indeed."

CHAPTER 17

THE TRAFFIC STOP

The crew made their way back to the Lady Alabama, boarded, and got the ship back in the air.

"So, Jagger," Charlie began, "do you remember exactly where that puddle was that took you to Galaxy 10, System 4?"

"Yeah. Why?" asked Jagger.

"Well, I think that's going to be our quickest route. Don't you?"

"Well, uh…," Jagger tried to say, but Addison interrupted.

"Of course he's right, Jagger," she said. "And you have nothing to be afraid of... we've done this together once already, and this time we know where we're going."

"Yeah, but...," Jagger tried to speak, but was again interrupted. This time by Benny.

"What are you talking about, lady?" Benny directed at Addison. "Captain Jagger Jones has ice in his veins, has nerves of steel, is cool as a cucumber. He's not afraid of anything." Benny turned to Jagger and gave him a grin and a wink, like he'd just helped the captain out with the situation. Jagger gave a quick grin back, but didn't seem to be sincere.

"So," persisted Charlie, "where bouts is this puddle?"

Jagger, who looked defeated, replied, "It's about 2,000 miles above the orange moon of Tengboche," and he pointed to the other planet in the system with multiple moons. They could faintly see one orange, one blue, and one white moon, hovering around a planet that looked to be about four planets away.

"Well let's get moving," Lizzie chimed in.

Lady Alabama flew in a direct route towards Tengboche. As they passed the first planet between them and their destination, they began to have other spacecraft flying around. A little further along and there were lighted buoys lining a path which funneled all the ships to a check point.

"What's going on?" asked Lizzie.

"Traffic stop," answered Jagger anxiously. "This system likes to keep tabs on what and who is coming in and out of this area. Just let me do the talking."

When they got up to the front of the check point, a spacecraft with a red light flashing on its top like a police car was positioned directly in front of them. The craft was at least five times as large as the Lady Alabama. It was large, silver, and had lots of congruent, rounded edges, that reminded Charlie of muscles on a body builder. A voice rang out over a speaker, "Name of craft?"

"The Lady Alabama," answered Jagger.

Immediately the voice rang out again, "Name of captain?"

Jagger hesitated slightly and then answered, "Micah Tortoiseshell."

The crew looked around at each other as if to ask with their eyes, "What is going on?"

Right then, before any of them could ask about the false name Jagger Jones had given, a bright, flat, red light shone through the windshield and moved swiftly downward across Jagger's face. It was obvious that this caught Jagger by surprise and he began to look more anxious than ever. A computerized voice announced, "Retinal scan completed." Immediately, the one red flashing light on the craft turned into thirty red, blue, and yellow flashing lights. The voice rang out once again, this time louder than ever, "Jagger Jones, you are wanted for owed debt to the Grand Baron. Prepare your ship for boarding."

Jagger turned to the rest of his crew and with one look and no words, said "I'm sorry" and "What do we do?"

Charlie flipped on the microphone from his co-pilot's seat and pleaded to the muscled ship, "Sir, I am sorry, but we need Captain Jones for our rescue mission. We promise we will return and tend to his owed debt once our mission is completed."

As Charlie spoke, a small ship was released from the larger ship and flew below the Lady to the airlock in the floor.

The voice replied, "Unacceptable. The Grand Baron has already been notified and has requested the prompt apprehension of Captain Jones."

Jagger gave Charlie a look of fear that Charlie had yet to see from his captain throughout their intense travels. They felt a bump of the small ship below them trying to dock and lock-in with the Lady's airlock.

The entire crew now looked at Charlie to decide what would happen next. With only a second of thought and hesitation, he turned his microphone back on, and said with intense calmness, "Unacceptable!"

He touched his control panel and the Lady rocked back and forth, knocking loose the ship below it. Jagger smiled and turned back toward the front of the ship, but before he could even grab onto his controls, Charlie lifted the ship above the silver, mammoth ship, and was on the move. Jagger grabbed hold and called out, "I'll take it from here, kiddo!"

Then, from the back Benny gave out a loud, "Giddy-up!", in his best Jagger voice.

They sped through space trying to stay in the direction of their destination. Quickly, however, three smaller ships headed toward them from their front. As they approached, the ships began firing lasers at the Lady Alabama. Jagger steered the ship this way and that, dodging the lasers, then turned the ship directly up to change their path. The three ships followed, along with the crowd of five ships that had gathered behind them.

The Lady Alabama was faster than the ships chasing it, but Jagger still had to maneuver the craft to dodge the star torpedoes and lasers that were being fired at them. He went up and down, left and right, at one point even did a corkscrew maneuver that dodged one of the torpedoes. Unfortunately, at this point they were off their path toward the orange moon of Tengboche. Jagger knew if it were as simple as outrunning the mob of silver, laser firing ships to the puddle, he'd have no trouble at all, but since they were between the Lady and their destination, he'd have to come up with something clever.

Jagger headed for the nearest planet, which was blue and tan colored. "I've got a plan!" he yelled out.

The speed of the Lady had created a little distance between them and their pursuers, by the time they reached the planet. Jagger went straight into the atmosphere of the planet and flew directly for the blue… water.

They barely even slowed down, as they dove nose first into the ocean. With Charlie hard at work as co-pilot, he quickly got the Lady's submarine mode functioning. They continued going deeper into the water until they were a couple hundred feet down, and Jagger brought the ship to an idle.

Everything was quiet for a few seconds, and then Professor Hootie asked, "This is Filipany, isn't it?"

"Say what now?" replied Jagger, obviously rattled by the chase, and uncertain why the professor would care where they were at this point.

"This planet we are on... it's Filipany. No?"

"Uh...," Jagger thought about it for a few seconds, "Yeah. Yeah, I think so," he replied unsure of the significance.

"And you're not worried about the gillawatts?"

"The who and the what now?" Jagger now sounded confused and concerned.

"The gillawatts. You know, the giant sea creatures that inhabit the oceans of Filipany. They are like giant, electric eels that are said to be able to produce one billion volts of electricity, which is essentially the same as a bolt of lightning. They typically grow to about three hundred feet long. If I recall properly," the professor paused to sift through some of his brain's files and confirm the information he was about to tell the pilot, "these oceans are quite infested with them."

"Well," said Jagger trying to stay calm and keep everyone else that way as well, "we only need to stay down here for just a few minutes. That'll give enough time for the Grand Baron's ships to get onto the planet. Then we can leave, and out-fly them to where the puddle is. Besides these oceans are huge, I'd say the chances of us encountering a gillawatt are pretty slim."

As he spoke the last word with his back to the ship's windshield and facing the rest of the ship's crew, he saw their eyes get big, and Lizzie lifted her right hand and pointed to the windshield. Jagger turned to see the tail-half of a gillawatt pass just ten feet away from the ship. Almost as soon as it's tail disappeared, the head reappeared, and it repeated this three more times, each time seemingly swimming faster. The Lady Alabama began to sink slightly in the water.

"He's circling us," stated Addison. "I think it's creating a whirlpool."

"He's trying to suck us down to the ocean floor," the professor announced. "I remember studying about this tactic. The swirling water calls more creatures to the area, and they attack better against the ocean floor."

Charlie chimed in, "Yeah, well not on my watch. Jagger we're getting out of here. Hope it's been long enough," and he worked at his controls and tipped the ship's nose upward toward the surface.

They could really start feeling the pull of the circling water at this point, and the ship was definitely beginning to sink. Two more gillawatts came into view, swimming well above them, but coming in their direction. One coming from their left and one from their right.

Charlie got the engines going strong and he yelled up to Jagger, "Steer us out of here, Captain!"

Jagger pushed the throttle forward, and they began speeding toward the surface. The gillawatt that had been circling them began to chase them from behind. The other two began swimming faster trying to cut off the ship's angle to the water's surface. Jagger held his course heading straight upward, with the three beasts converging on them. With only about thirty feet to go, Jagger realized the gillawatt coming at them from the right was going to get to them before they could exit the ocean. It opened its large mouth wide and exposed ten rows of small, sharp teeth. Jagger quickly veered left and spun, and the creature missed the ship by only a few feet. But this slowed them down ever so much, allowing the other two beasts to gain some ground on the ship.

The Lady reached the surface and burst out of the water with the other two gillawatts hot on their trail, both bursting out of the water as well. A hundred feet of their bodies simultaneously surging from the water after the little, sleek, white ship, but missing it by only a couple of feet. And though they missed the ship, they did not miss hitting each other, which caused them both to create an electrical blast which radiated across the water and sounded like a huge clap of thunder.

The crew of course was extremely happy they had not been eaten or electrocuted, but the happiness quickly faded as the loud clap from the electrical blast and the flash of radiating light, alerted all of the Grand Baron's ships, which had been flying over the desert areas of Filipany, to the location of Captain Jagger Jones and his accomplices. The silver, muscled ships abruptly changed their direction, and took back chase with the Lady Alabama. Jagger, however, felt confident that with this head start, he would be able to beat his pursuers to their destination.

Back into space, they sped as fast as they could toward the orange moon of Tengboche. They had gained enough of a lead to avoid being fired upon, but were still in view of the mob of muscle-bound ships.

When Jagger felt they were near the area, they, themselves, began firing the Lady's laser cannon into space. And finally, they saw it... a ripple. A ripple in space... a puddle. Without even slowing, they flew straight into the middle of it.

To the Grand Baron's men, they just vanished. Out in the distance, but right in front of their eyes, the entire spacecraft had just disappeared.

To the crew of the Lady Alabama, everything went black.

Chapter 18

Galaxy 10, System 4

Free falling ensued, then the sliding and the tie-dyed swirling lights. The crew seemed to enjoy this puddle jump much more than the previous one. Charlie and Lizzie actually had smiles on their faces, and Benny... well Benny screamed, "Woohoo!" and then, "Yeah, Baby!" as the ship dipped and turned. Lastly, came the swirling and... POP. They were once again in space.

Benny let out an, "Aww," as if the ride had not lasted long enough.

All the Lady's navigational equipment had once again gone out, and the first thing they noticed through the windshield was that no planets could be seen, only lots of stars in the distance.

"So which way?" Charlie asked Jagger.

"Not really sure," replied Jagger, "I kind of flew around aimlessly for three weeks the last time. Not sure which direction I headed in first."

"Well, we can't be out here three weeks," Lizzie stated concerned. "We have to get to mom and dad before that. They must be so scared."

"No, I know," comforted Jagger, "and it won't take that. Since I know the galaxy and system we are in, I should be able to manually reset the Lady's navigational systems and she'll let us know the way to Castor and Pollux."

"Any chance we get company from the Grand Baron's crew?" Addison asked.

"Doubtful," stated Jagger. "Cats from Galaxy 7, System 3 are pretty much homebodies… never leave their system. Not sure what the deal is. But, I do know if you went to Nucleus or Earth, which I think you'd all agree are the two biggest melting pot planets in the universe, you won't find any Boxchoxies, Tengbochites, Filipanies, or any other species from that system. But," he continued, "just in case, I think I'll put a little distance between us and this puddle for the time being."

Once he felt he had cleared the area enough, Jagger began working on resetting the navigational systems of the Lady Alabama. As he did so, Addison was the first to speak up and ask the question they'd all been wondering, "So, what was all that about back there?" she directed to their captain.

"What was *what* all about?" Jagger pretended not to know what she was talking about.

"Um, the lights, the sirens, the torpedoes that nearly killed us?"

"Ooooh, right," Jagger said as if she'd jogged his memory. "You know me, Addy. It was a long time ago. And man-oh-man, do those guys hold grudges."

"Yeah they do. But what I'm asking is what was that grudge all about?" Addison prodded further.

"Like I said, it was a long time ago. I was younger… dumber… felt like I could take on the world," stated Jagger.

"You hustled them, didn't you?" said Charlie. "Like the guys you told me about on Mars."

"Well, not exactly," replied Jagger as he continued to work on the Lady's navigation systems. "Actually, I lost. You're correct that it was a race. At the time, I had never been beaten. So, maybe I wagered a bit more than I had, but I just thought there was no way I'd lose. Boy, was I wrong. The Grand Baron had a pilot flying against me who was good, he was very good, and had a brand new, very fast ship. And Bella… well… Bella had a few miles on her to say the least. I tried to cut some time by flying close to the planet we were circling and I clipped the atmosphere which slowed me down even more."

"Classic rookie mistake," Charlie interjected to give Jagger a hard time. Everyone laughed.

"Right?" said Jagger. "I never should have done that, but I still finished in second place of eight flyers," he looked around to see the impressed looks on his friends' faces, but got none. "Anyway," he said, "only first place got the prize money and everyone else had to pay up. And like I said before, the pay out was much more than I had, but I never planned on having to pay it. I gave them what I had, but it wasn't good enough. I told the

168

Grand Baron I'd work off the rest of the debt, but he said he was going to throw me into prison instead. And, well, this turtle wasn't made for hard time, so I bailed. Gave them a good chase. Flew Bella like I'd never flown her before… shoulda flown her like that in the race and I wouldn't have been in that mess," he said diverting from the story, then shook his head and continued, "anyway, torpedo missed me, I saw a ripple, and you all know the rest of the story."

"Galaxy 10, System 4," stated Charlie, sort of finishing Jagger's thoughts.

"Yep," Jagger confirmed, "and here we are again. Funny how life sometimes comes full circle like that." He made one final twist of a lever, and pushed a button. Then, went back to his captain's chair. Typed in the number "10", and then "4". Hit "Enter", and the Lady Alabama's navigational equipment began working once again. Jagger set the course for Castor and Pollux and they were off.

It took a day and a half before the two planets came into view. From a distance, they almost looked as if they were still connected. They had the appearance of a short-handled dumbbell, with two gray, round ends and a small, cylindrical protrusion that connected the two. As they got closer, however, a black line, that was the darkness of space, could be seen separating the two. It was like the "handle" of the "dumbell" had been sliced down the middle.

"So, where to?" asked Benny as they got even closer. "Castor, or Pollux?"

"Either's just as cold and barren as the other if you ask me," replied Jagger, having second thoughts if they had deciphered the clue from Boxchox's ringed moon properly.

"I was thinking about that," started Addison, "remember what the first part of the clue said **'where a meteor incised and one became two**'? Well, I think we have to go to the 'incision site'." She put her hands in the air and made quotation marks with her fingers as she said the phrase "incision site".

"I agree with Dr. Fox," chimed in Lizzie. "I'm not sure whether it's Castor or Pollux, but I think we have to go in to where the meteor separated them."

The others agreed, and Jagger steered the ship straight for the dark line between the two. As they approached, they began to see color from the flat protrusion areas of the planets. No one color in particular, but just color which contrasted against the vast gray-white of the rest of the frozen planets. This sign of life, gave Jagger a little more hope that they had in fact interpreted the clue correctly.

"That's crazy," stated Jagger as they had now gotten between the two planets and could actually see some vegetation at their surfaces. "How? When the rest of the planet is so frozen... how?" he asked with a voice of perplexed amazement. He said it, but they were all thinking it.

Then the professor spoke up, "The meteor," he said. They all looked at him not understanding, so he continued. "It must have heated the core enough... when it split the two... the friction," he was still working his theory out in his head, "a spark... a spark of life and enough heat to sustain it... mix it with the trace amount of heat they get from their small sun," he pointed out in the distance at a small, red sun, which Charlie and Liz thought looked like a dying flame on a candle. "The heat from the sun and the heat of the core, and..."

"And," he was interrupted by Charlie, "the perfect hideout for pirates is born."

CHAPTER 19

THE INCISION SITE

They took the Lady down onto the "incision site" of Castor first, and did a quick fly around. It was beautiful. Colors everywhere. Coral everywhere. Yes, that's right, the whole incision area of Castor looked like the ocean floor of a Caribbean paradise, except that it was not under water and everything was bigger. Projecting high into the air, were stalks of leafy kelp* which swayed in the breeze, but looked as if water was passing across them. Unlike an ocean floor, there were also clusters of tall, large bamboo chutes that were dispersed among the coral, but they did not seem out of place at all. At the base of the bamboo clusters, were beautifully colored flowers, and adhered to the side of the brilliant green chutes, they could see sparkling colorful bead-like structures. The surface of the planet appeared to be sand, but it was difficult to distinguish between all the colorful coral rock formations, the clusters of large green bamboo, the tall leafy kelp stalks, and the large plant-like colorful anemones*, the latter two of which both moved in the air as if they had a life of their own.

They flew around for about an hour, covering most of the inhabitable area of Castor. As gorgeous as the scenery was, the crew saw nothing that gave them reason to stop and land, so they continued on toward the incision site of Pollux.

As one would imagine, the surface of Pollux's incision site was identical to that of Castor's, after all... they were twins. Again, they flew and gazed at the beauty of the area, with it's swaying kelp stalks and anemones, which were almost hypnotic. The crew had to focus on keeping their eyes peeled, searching for a clue. About thirty minutes into their fly-by of Pollux, Lizzie first spotted it.

"There!" she exclaimed. "To the right. Do you see it?"

They did. Looking like a decoration at the bottom of an aquarium, they saw a pirate ship sitting, parked, on the surface of Pollux. Though it looked like a normal pirate ship, with sails, a wooden hull, and even cannons hanging out of the sides, the crew knew that this was actually a high-tech spacecraft that was used to rob and kidnap. Chills went down the spines of the two teenagers who knew they were getting close to confronting their parents' captors.

"Think I'll park this thing a little bit away from the Jolly Roger there," stated Jagger. "I'm thinking we're gonna want to keep the Lady hidden."

"Good idea," agreed the professor, and the rest of the crew nodded in agreement as well. So, Jagger landed the ship behind a large coral rock formation with two large orange anemones sitting on it. They were a hundred yards away from the pirate ship.

It wasn't until now Jagger realized that without Marvin with them, HE was going to have to stay back with the ship. Charlie was really the only other crew member who could fly it, and he knew there was zero point zero chance he was talking Charlie into staying behind. Plus, he also knew from past experiences that Charlie was more valuable to the team with his martial arts abilities. Jagger removed his small holster and laser pistol from his right boot, and handed it to Addison.

"Here," he said, "you might need this."

With this statement, it dawned on the others that Jagger would not be able to come with them, but also the seriousness of the situation which lay ahead.

"I'll be just an ear shot away," Jagger stated as he removed his wristband and handed it to Charlie. Then Jagger put on a headset with microphone and earpiece. "Good luck."

The large door at the rear of the ship lowered into a ramp, and the crew exited. Benny was the last one off the ship. Before he exited, Jagger stopped him and said very seriously, "Look after them, bro."

Benny, hovering in the air, stood up straight, saluted his captain with one of his six little legs, and said very military like, "Sir, yes, sir!" Jagger smiled and nodded, which seemed to release

Benny from his frozen salute, and he followed the rest of the crew out into the beauty that was Pollux.

Indeed the surface was covered in sand, as they had thought, but a hard surface was just below it, so that their feet did not sink as they walked. They weaved through the paths around the large coral formations, heading toward the pirate ship... staying alert. As she walked, Lizzie felt she saw a flittering in her peripheral vision. But when she turned to see what was there... there was nothing... only coral, and the flittering was gone.

She wasn't the only one. They all had an eerie feeling, like they were being watched. About halfway to the pirate ship they came upon their first cluster of the large green bamboo chutes. It was now clear to them that the colorful flowers at the base of the clusters were two foot tall pitcher plants* that were a foot in diameter. They looked like large, colorful vases with lids. They did not

178

originate from the ground, but instead were attached to the base of the bamboo by vines from which they grew. Each of the lids at this particular cluster of plants were closed.

The crew paused here, and looked up the large chutes at the sparkling bead-like structures, which from this closer range, they could see the were a sort of glittery cocoon.

As they were about to continue forward, something happened… something that caused them to pause once more. One of the lids of the pitcher plants began to open.

CHAPTER 20

MYTH BECOMES TRUE

The lid of a bright red pitcher plant slowly opened. The crew waited with anxious anticipation, as they could now see something moving from inside the plant. Addison put her hand near her leg, ready to draw her laser pistol if need be. The lid fully opened. In an instant, out flew a small creature that was eight inches tall, and its body was a shiny, metallic silver, that reminded them of liquid mercury*. It was human shaped, with two wings attached to the sides of its back like a butterfly. The wings were mostly sheer white, outlined in the same silver as the being's body, and covered with fantastically ornate silver patterns. It's hair was snow-white and grew upward into a flattop. It wore only one article of clothing… a white apron with a pocket in the front.

The crew was mesmerized by the image in front of them, and now caught more flittering in their periphery, but this time when they turned to look, the flittering did not disappear. Instead, they saw at least fifty more of these beings hovering around them.

"Helloooo," the tiny creature that had emerged from the pitcher plant said in a goofy, male, strongly Norwegian accent. "My name is Inger. Can I help youuu?"

"Inger, you say?" asked Dr. Fox

"That is right. It is like 'a finger', but it is Inger."

"Well, Inger," Addison continued, "pardon me if I am being offensive here, but I am a specialist in alien medicine and know the anatomy of over 3,000 species of aliens, and I just can't come up with what species you are."

"No offense, pretty lady, but it's because we are not aliens."

Confused she asked, "Then what are you?"

"Well...," he flittered about just a bit and flew even closer to Dr. Fox, "We're fairies of course," and he continued, "and not just any fairies, we are tooth fairies."

Charlie chirped up, "Wait a second... like for real tooth fairies? Like leave money under your pillow tooth fairies?"

"Yup. That is us. That's what our aprons are for. They have these handy-dandy pockets to carry money in when we visit a planet, and we carry the little teethies in the same pocket when we return home. Handy-dandy don't you think?" Inger said as he put his hands into the pocket of the apron to show off the carrying space.

"Uh, yeah," replied Charlie, "very nice."

"Handy-dandy," corrected Inger.

"Yes, very handy-dandy," stated Charlie trying not to upset the tooth fairy. Then like a light switch had gone off in his head, Charlie blurted out, "It was bamboo!"

"Excuse me?" asked Inger.

"What are you talking about, B.B.?" inquired Lizzie.

"You know the sign... on the moon... 'We have moved'... the sign... it was bamboo," he stated, then continued, "it all makes sense... all those baby teeth all over the moon of Boxchox, and that out-of-place wooden sign, and now you... here... with these totally big bamboo chutes."

"Yah," started Inger, "I take it you visited our old home, and you got our note?"

"And you guys are the last part of the clue, aren't you?" asked Lizzie.

"That's right," chimed in Professor Hootie who had been oddly quiet this whole time and was just trying to process the events and information he was currently obtaining. "Where a meteor incised and one became two, **a species does live and myth becomes true**," he emphasized the second half of the sentence. "You all are the myth."

"Yaaaahh," stated Inger excitedly flittering around in a circle while clapping his hands and then exclaiming, "And we are true!"

"You sure are," commented Benny. "So I have to ask, why did you move?"

"Are you kidding me?" Inger spoke. "Look at this place! Do you remember what that dreadful moon looked like? Dark. Scenery was not nearly as good. This place is beautiful, and we don't have to use the teethies to build things any more."

"Yeah, the teeth," Lizzie began, "where are the…" and she was interrupted by a loud tearing sound which came from above them. They all turned their attention upward. Thirty feet up one of the oversized bamboo chutes, a purple and turquoise chrysalis*, which looked like it had been doused in silver glitter, was being torn open from the inside. A little silver fairy with long, flowing snow-white hair emerged, and began flying. At first, she flew around wobbling a bit, like a bird with a wounded wing, but a few seconds later she got the hang of it and went flittering off across the coral area, spiraling around a tall kelp stalk, and flew out of site.

"Juniper got her wings today," stated Inger with affection. "They grow up so fast," he said, and got a little choked up.

The crew marveled at the event, and when she felt enough time had passed Lizzie continued,

"So I was asking about the teeth you all collect… where do you put them if you are not using them to build things?"

"Oh, yah, all the teethies go in the teethies pit. We now collect them for Mr. Goldtoothie. I guess you could say it is like our rent for living here. Have I told you how much we like living here?"

"You mentioned it," replied Benny.

"You know Goldtooth?" Charlie quickly asked. "You know where he is?"

"Yah, most likely I'm a knowing," stated Inger. "So what are you all wanting with Mr. Goldtoothie anyways?"

"He took our mom and dad," said Lizzie. "We just came to get them back."

"Oh no," said Inger truly concerned. "I'm sure it has something to do with that potion he concocts. You know he really is a pretty nice man…

most of the times, but uh sometimes he gets a little bit crazy when it comes to that potion he concocts. He's always nice to us unless he thinks we are bringing him too many of the teethies with the cavities in them. Like it is our fault if the kiddies have gotten cavities in their teethies, but he says he can't have the cavities getting into that potion he concocts or it will poison him good."

"Yeah," said Lizzie, "that's where our parents come into the picture. They are both dentists, and we believe Goldtooth is using them to determine which teeth are cavity free, and can be used in his potion."

"Oh no," said Inger again, "that is not good because he gets a bit crazy about that potion he concocts."

"Yeah," blurted out Benny, "you mentioned that."

Inger continued, "Well I don't know, but they are your parents and Mr. Goldtoothie shouldn't have just taken them like that. And you've come all this way, and well, we will just have to help you all in anyways we can."

"I think telling us where we can find Goldtooth is a good start," replied Charlie.

Right then, he heard Jagger's voice come through his wristband, "Hey Chuck, what's going on out there? Give me an update, dude."

Charlie raised the wristband to his mouth and pressed a button, "Chill out, man. We were just about to get some info on Goldtooth and his crew from a tooth fairy."

Jagger quickly replied, "Oh, okay, cool... wait what?" as he realized the oddity of Charlie's statement. Charlie quickly put the wristband on mute so as to not be interrupted again.

"You were saying?" he directed toward Inger.

"You have to be careful, but you will want to go in this direction," and he pointed past where the pirate ship was, "then you will see the teethies pit. You will want to cross over that bridge, and then you will come to a opening in a large blue coral rock. You'll have to go in, but this is where you really have to be careful, because they say that Mr. Goldtoothie has set up a series of booby-traps on the way in to his laboratory where he brews up that potion he concocts."

"Any idea of what type of booby-traps we're talking here?" asked Professor Hootie.

"I'm a having no clue."

"How many men would you say are in Goldtooth's pirate crew?" asked Benny. The rest of the crew seemed impressed with his question, and

Benny said calmly, "We need to know what we're up against." They agreed.

Inger began, "Oh, let's see now, I'd say not counting Mr. Goldtoothie himself," he began counting on his tiny silver fingers. "Let's see, there's **Hook-hand Harry** and **Peg-leg Larry**, there's **One-eyed Walter** and **Four-fingered Freddy**, there's **Scarneck**, **Sharkbite**, **Frank the Plank**, and… **Kyle**. So, what's that? Eight? Yah, I'd say there's eight… not counting Mr. Goldtoothie."

"Well," started Benny, "that was more information than I needed."

"Ok, well," started Charlie, "does anyone else have any questions before we go?" They all looked around at each other and shrugged their shoulders and shook their heads. Charlie spoke again, "Thank you, Mr. Inger, for your help, and I hope we'll see you again real soon."

"It truly was a pleasure," stated the professor, and they all said goodbye and were on their way.

The five of them continued on their path, and had only taken a few steps when they heard another ripping sound. They paused, looked back, and saw another chrysalis, this one pink and green and glittering silver, tearing apart. Another young fairy was awkwardly attempting to fly for the first time, but just like before, she seemed to perfect the act in only a few moments.

CHAPTER 21

THE BRIDGE AND THE DOOR

They continued ahead and quickly approached the space pirate ship. As they did, Charlie nudged Lizzie and pointed to the very back of the ship, which had a large bumper sticker stuck to it that read: "You can't handle the **TOOTH**!" All the words were written in black, except for the word "tooth" which was written in gold. Charlie and Lizzie both found this amusing and laughed just a bit, but then immediately felt guilty about thinking their parents' captor was humorous.

There was no one present at the ship, so the five of them continued following the sandy path through the beautiful coral. After walking another half a mile, they could see an area ahead of them where the ground stopped, as if they were approaching a deep ravine. They walked to the edge, and with no doubt in their minds, they had reached "the teethies pit", as Inger had called it. There was really no way to tell how deep the pit was, because of all the baby teeth that were piled into it, but it must have been a good fifty yards wide. To Charlie, it reminded him of a large silo* of grain or corn, but with teeth instead.

With prickly, dense coral on either side of them, there was no path around the pit, nor was it needed, because just as Inger had told them, there was a bridge that stretched across the entirety of the pit. They could see the large, sparkling, blue rock he had described just on the other side. The bridge was made of bamboo, and was only a foot wide. Of course Professor Hootie and Benny flew right over it, but Charlie, Lizzie, and Dr. Fox walked carefully out onto the narrow bridge.

There was a thirty foot drop from the bridge to the peak of the piled up teeth. Charlie and Lizzie, with their impeccable balance from their martial arts and gymnastics training crossed with ease, never really taking notice of how high up they were. Addison on the other hand was taking the trek quite slowly and was trying hard not to look down. She had gotten to about the middle of the bridge when she stalled a bit. Then, seemingly out of nowhere, three of the tooth fairies quickly flew near her in order to make a deposit of teeth into the pit. This startled the beautiful, young doctor and the others watched nervously as she began to lose her balance. Professor Hootie quickly took to the air toward her, but she began to fall backward off the bridge, before he could reach her.

However, before she came completely off the bridge, her body stopped falling. The three fairies had seen her as they emptied their apron pockets, and had flown into action. With one fairy under each of her shoulders, and another in the center of her back, the three tiny beings, were able to stabilize Addison. Professor Hootie quickly reached her, wrapped his taloned feet around her shoulders, and airlifted her the rest of the way to the other side of "the teethies pit."

"So sorry, if we startled you," said one of the the three fairies with the same Norwegian accent as Inger. "We were not expecting to see you here."

"We don't get many visitors," said one of the others.

"No, no," started Addison, "thank you for saving me there. I don't think those teeth would have felt good embedded into my back," she half joked, but also was half serious.

They all giggled, and then one said, "I like you." Then, they quickly turned and flew away.

"Peculiar little buggers, aren't they?" stated the professor.

"Yeah," said Benny, "I mean what are they so happy about all the time?"

Charlie put his wristband up to his mouth, pushed a button and said, "Jagger, we are about to go into a cave that should lead us to Goldtooth's lab, so stand by."

"Roger that, Charlie dude," came Jagger's voice. "Y'all be careful in there, ya hear?"

"Roger that," Charlie replied.

They entered the opening at the base of the large, sparkling, blue rock which was really more like a small mountain. They walked forward only ten feet and found themselves inside a large cavernous room with an arched ceiling of natural white crystals. The sunlight must have been reaching the crystals from the outside, because they illuminated the room wondrously. It was like they had entered a capital building, or cathedral, and were in the most beautiful rotunda* they had ever seen. They couldn't help but marvel for a short moment at the ceiling and the cave in general, but then they looked around for where to go next. There was really only one option. There was a door on the other side of the domed room, straight across from where they were.

Remembering what the tooth fairy had said about booby-traps, the five of them studied the floor and the walls as they proceeded forward with great caution. They saw nothing outside the ordinary until they reached the door.

It was a large wooden door, likely made from the oversized bamboo which adorned the planet. Directly in the center of the door, there was a keyhole. There were four etchings above the keyhole which ran in a vertical pattern:

To the right of the door, on the wall were mounted five keys, all which had unique designs at the handle portion of the key.

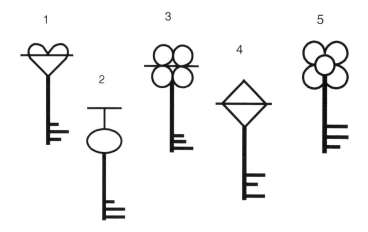

"Well," started Charlie, "I guess we have to figure out which key to use, huh?"

"That's what I'm assuming," replied the professor.

(Which key do YOU think is the one?)

"Question is," Addison said, "what happens if we choose the wrong one?"

This brought another level of seriousness to the group and they began to concentrate on the etched images to see what pattern they could find. They stood in silence five feet away from the door and the keys, so that they could see them all in one view, each trying to make something of the images.

"I got nothin'," Benny said after a couple of minutes, breaking the silence.

Charlie stated, "I just keep thinking about suits in a deck of cards; hearts," he pointed to the image that looked like a heart with a line under it, "and clubs," he pointed to the image just below it that looked like a four-leafed clover with no stem. "And that key there," he then pointed to the fourth key on the wall, "That looks like a diamond with a line through it."

The others agreed, but were not sold on this being the answer yet.

"What about the other two images?" Addison asked. "How do they play into your 'deck of cards' theory?"

"Not real sure," admitted Charlie. "Maybe they are houses?" he said with a definite level of uncertainty. "A full house is a hand in cards, sooooo… maybe?"

"Those are the two, I'm focusing more on," stated the professor speaking of the first and fourth etched images. "They seem to be the same figure with only the horizontal line having changed positions."

"Yes," said Addison, "and then there is the key," and she pointed to first key, "that looks like a heart with only the horizontal line raised, as well."

"Indeed," stated Professor Hootie.

Lizzie remained silent having heard the others, but still concentrating on the images and their possible patterns from afar.

"So," Charlie asked, "you guys think that's the one?" He paused waiting for a confirmation, but got silence from the others. No one was confident enough in their suggestions to speak up. "Well, we can't stand here all day, and it sounds like it's two against one for the heart over the diamond."

Charlie stepped forward from the group and went to the wall facing the keys. He took a deep breath, and reached his hand toward the first key in the group that looked like a heart with a line through it.

As he did, Lizzie, from her spot five feet away, raised her left hand fully extended out in front of her face, and then closed her left eye... and she saw it.

Charlie clutched the heart shaped key and pulled it off the wall. As he did, he heard Lizzie shout, "B.B., NO!"

As if it were happening in slow motion, he realized a string was attached to the key as he pulled it from the wall, and he heard a faint sound of a release, and then something whizzing through the air. But, before whatever it was could reach him, Lizzie hit him first, and tackled him to the ground.

Charlie was slightly embarrassed about the linebacker-like shot he'd just taken from his little sister, and now her body draped on his. But other than a little bit of ego, he was happy to realize that he had not been hurt by whatever contraption had been set into motion by the key. However, that happiness was quick lived as he began to roll Lizzie from off the top of himself, "Get off me, you nut," he said.

"Stop! Don't move her!" Dr. Fox said as her emergency room skills kicked in. Addison quickly ran over and slid her arms underneath Lizzie, who was lying face down on top of Charlie, and seemed limp. Stabilizing her body, Addison raised Lizzie slightly, and directed Professor Hootie, "Get him out of there."

Professor Hootie grabbed Charlie's arms and pulled him out from under his sister. Charlie then jumped to his feet and turned toward Lizzie. He now saw what the sense of panic was about. Lizzie was lying face down on the cave's floor with an arrow sticking straight out of her back. He had flashbacks of her lying unconscious on the ground in the woods behind their house with a Muzz Bug stuck into her fanny, and images of her lying peacefully on the energy bed of the Lady Alabama, nearly dead.

Dr. Fox quickly ripped open the back of Lizzie's shirt from where the arrow had gone through. When she did, she jumped back just a bit with a look of confusion. The arrowhead was imbedded into Lizzie's back, and from around the puncture wound, where Dr. Fox expected to see crimson blood trickling, was an oozing of a green substance.

Addison quickly shook off her surprise and said, "We have to pull the arrow out. It looks as though it might have hit her spine. Hold her," she directed. Charlie took a step backward and had a look of disbelief on his face. After all they had been through in the past week trying to save his sister, and now, here, in this cave, she lies with an arrow in her spine, once again, seemingly lifeless.

Professor Hootie stepped forward and held Lizzie, and Dr. Fox placed her left hand near the puncture site and stabilized herself. With her right hand she grabbed the shaft of the arrow and she pulled. Addison was glad that Lizzie was unconscious for this part because she knew that if she wasn't, the pain would almost be unbearable. The barbs of the arrow's tip resisted in Lizzie's flesh, but Dr. Fox was able to get it out without too much trouble. The arrowhead dripped with the thick, green, blood-like substance as Addison removed it. This caught Charlie's eye, and out of curiosity he moved closer to his sister to see what was going on. The puncture wound now slowly oozed more of the green.

Addison ripped off the left sleeve of her own shirt in order to compress it on the wound. "We have to stop the bleeding," she said. But before she could begin, the green ooze, coming out of Lizzie's wound began to form a bubble. Addison stopped what she was doing briefly to try to figure out what was going on. Charlie, Professor Hootie, and Benny were all looking on with completely flabbergasted looks on their faces. They moved in even closer to watch this weird phenomenon. It looked as if Lizzie's back had blown a bubble with some bright, neon-green bubble gum. As they watched, and the bubble got bigger, they realized the wound was constricting and getting smaller. All four of them leaned in even closer to make sure they were seeing this correctly. Then, when the bubble got to about the size of a bowling ball... *pop*!

The thick slimy green substance from the bubble splattered all over the onlookers' faces, and through the slime, they could see that the arrow's wound was completely healed. They were then, even more surprised by the next sound they heard.

"Five!" shouted Lizzie, who was still lying face down.

Charlie, Addison, and Professor Hootie began removing the green goop from their faces, and Benny, whose whole body had gotten covered, flew around and shook like a wet dog slinging the slime around the empty cave.

"What?" Charlie asked, having almost forgotten why they were even where they were.

"Five," repeated Lizzie, as she stood to her feet and dusted herself off like nothing had happened. They all looked at her like she was a ghost.

Charlie, with mixed emotions, one of which was amusement at his little sister, said, "Umm, you just took an arrow to the back... for me, I might add... so thank you... there, I said that... and now you just jump up and say 'Five, five'. We have no idea what you are even talking about. We thought you were dead."

"I think she means, the fifth key, Charlie," suggested Professor Hootie. "So you think, it's the one that looks like a flower, Lizzie? What brings you to that conclusion?"

"No," stated Lizzie, "not the fifth key." This statement took the professor off guard. "The number five. Look," and she went to face the door, put her forearm over the left half of the images etched into the door, and there it was clear as day for them all to see... the numbers 1,2,3, and 4 in order going down. She then reached over and with her hand, covered the left half of the second key, which again very clearly was the number 5. She grabbed the key, took it from the wall, inserted it into the keyhole of the large wooden door, and gave it a turn. The door opened.

Chapter 22

The Bookcase Booby-trap

Beyond the door, was a long, dark hallway.

Charlie used a flashlight feature on Jagger's wristband to light the way, and they all proceeded with extreme caution.

As they walked slowly, looking all around Charlie spoke, "So, Dr. Fox, how could that have happened... with Lizzie? I mean... have you ever seen that before?"

"No, never," she replied. "I'm not real sure what to make of it."

"The green," the professor stated calmly. They all turned to look at him, and he continued,

"I've been thinking about it, and well… it has to be the green water from the waterfall on Nangu'n. Don't you think?"

The others contemplated what the professor was saying, and as they did, he continued to make his case. "First off there's the color… the water was green, and now her blood… or what ever that is, is also green. Secondly, it healed her once, from the muzz. Maybe… and just hear me out here, but maybe that green water was not so much an 'anti-venom'," he put air quotes around the phrase, "as it was a 'cure-all'," and he did the same with that one. "Maybe, just maybe it gave Lizzie the power to heal herself… from anything."

"So you're saying I'm a superhero?" said Lizzie very matter-of-factly.

They all laughed a little, except for Professor Hootie. When they realized he wasn't laughing, they stopped laughing, and he said, "Maybe…

sorta… kinda." They all appeared to be in disbelief, and then he said, "I mean, how should I know? Maybe this was a one time event, or maybe it has a sort of expiration date, where it will run it's course, so I definitely don't think we need to be testing it out."

Lizzie then grabbed Charlie's arm, pushed the button on his wristband, and spoke into it, "Hey Jagger, guess what?"

"Hey little Lizzie, that you?" returned Jagger's voice. "Everything okay?"

"Yeah," she answered. "Oh, and I'm a superhero," she blurted out partially joking and partially not. Charlie yanked his arm away from her, as she grinned back at him.

"Say what?" came Jagger's response obviously confused by the proclamation.

Charlie quickly replied, "Don't worry about it. We'll tell you later," and he ended the communication with Jagger.

Charlie found himself being a bit jealous of Lizzie's newly discovered, possible superpower. As I mentioned long ago, there was quite the sibling rivalry between these two.

Right about that time, the hallway came to a dead end. The crew could no longer move forward, and through the light coming from Charlie's wristband, they could see that the path had ended with a bookcase.

This was a very different bookcase than the one they had encountered at the secret lair of the T.U.S.K. That one was huge and filled with books. This one, in contrast, was about six feet tall, with only four shelves, and only five books, which were spread out on the shelves so that none was really near another.

First they looked around to see if there were any other ways to get out of this corridor, but they saw nothing. So, next Charlie decided to hold his light near the books to see what they were.

As he read the spines of the first two, he said, "Hey guys, I think this is another test."

"Another booby-trap, you mean," said Benny.

"Yeah, probably," Charlie replied, "but one we have to get past."

"Ahh," said Lizzie in a voice trying to sound mysterious, "it's the ol' secret passage behind a bookcase trick. I've seen this in lots of old movies. and cartoons. One of these books is the secret one that will make the bookcase spin open, revealing a hidden room on the other side. We just have to determine which book is the correct one, because if we choose poorly, B.B.," she emphasized, and directed her comment toward her big brother, giving him a little jab for his blunder at the wooden door, "we could all perish."

Charlie couldn't help but notice the newfound confidence in Lizzie's voice, now that she thought she just might be invincible. "Well," he said, "I think we'll let you be the one who chooses which book to pull on this time."

Then, they read the spines of all five books. The first, on the bottom shelf, leaning against the far left edge of the bookcase was **Treasure Island by Robert Louis Stevenson**. The second, on the second shelf, leaning against the left side of the middle partition of the bookcase was a book called **It's So Hard To Say Goodbye** written **by C.U. Later**. Book number three was also on the second shelf, but on the far right of the bookcase. It was titled **How to Avoid Repetitiveness**, and was authored **by Ben der Dundat**. The fourth book, was on the third shelf, and stood up straight midway between the left edge of the bookcase and the middle partition. It was called **How to Set Awesome Booby-traps** by **A.U. Mug**. And the last of the five books sat on the top shelf and leaned inward against the right side of the middle partition. On it's spine read the title **Knock Knock Jokes by Dr. Hoosether**.

They all studied the titles, and read, and re-read them to themselves over and over. Then they began to discuss.

(Which book do YOU think is the one?)

"I kind of hate to say it," stated Charlie, "but whoever put these here had a pretty good sense of humor."

"Yeah," said Lizzie, "obviously, all these aren't real books. Most of these titles and authors are made up."

"Well," said Addison, "I think we can all agree that **Treasure Island** IS a real book, and that it was indeed written by **Robert Louis Stevenson**."

"For sure," said Charlie, "and it's a book about pirates, so I think we definitely have to keep that one in contention."

"Think I'm leaning toward it," inserted Lizzie.

"But I feel like we can throw out the **Knock Knock Jokes** one. I mean **Dr. Hoosether**, like 'Who's there?' Doesn't seem to have any relevance that I can think of," said Addison. The others agreed.

"And the same with **How to Avoid Repetitiveness by Ben der Dundat**," stated Charlie. "I mean it's pretty funny, 'been there done that'... Ben der Dundat... but I don't see any significance."

"Except that 'THE THE Universe's Secret Keepers' should read it," joked Lizzie, and they all chuckled.

"And this one," the professor pointed at the book titled **It's So Hard to Say Goodbye** by C.U. **Later**, "this one kind of gives me an eerie feeling, like something bad might happen, but nothing really jumping out at me."

"Maybe if Goldtooth was a big Boys 2 Men fan," stated Benny.

"Do what?" asked the professor.

"You know," Benny said, "the song by Boys 2 Men... the music group... *It's so hard to say goodbye to yesterday...*" he sang, then composed himself and cleared his throat. "An exploration mission to Tropia... years back... someone left some music... good stuff," and he stopped talking. The other crew members giggled.

"Yeah," Charlie jested, "I guess maybe the former professor, former member of the T.U.S.K., turned kidnapping pirate captain could be a huge Boys 2 Men fan, so maybe we should't discard that one as a possibility quite yet."

"What about this other one?" asked Lizzie pointing to the book spine that read **How to Make Awesome Booby-traps by A.U. Mug**.

"Another that gives me an eerie feeling," stated Professor Hootie.

"Haven't quite figured out what the author's name is supposed to mean, like the others," said Addison. "It doesn't seem to make a sentence… **A.U. Mug,**" she repeated to see if she heard anything.

"Could it be another real book, like **Treasure Island**?" Lizzie asked.

"I doubt it," said Professor Hootie, "but possibly."

"So," started Lizzie, "are we going with **Treasure Island** then? A book about pirates." She looked around and everyone was in agreement, but like at the wooden door, no one seemed very certain. "Okay, then. Why don't you guys move back and let me do this one?" Lizzie said, and they all somewhat hesitantly agreed.

The four of them kind of huddled together and backed a good six feet away from the bookcase. Lizzie stayed and leaned down to the bottom shelf where **Treasure Island** leaned against the left edge of the bookcase. She reached slowly out for it and whispered, "Let's see if we can make this baby spin."

Then, just as she put her hand onto the spine of the book, she heard, "WAIT!"

It was Benny's voice. He spoke again, "Wait just a second there little missy. Professor, what did you say that Goldtooth's real name was again?" he asked.

"Vardiman Goldstein," replied the professor, unsure of what the hovering bug was getting at.

"And professor," Benny barked as if he was interrogating a suspect in a crime, "what is another name for a large mug that people often drink beer or coffee out of?"

Now the professor, even more confused, thought a second and answered with uncertainty, "A stein?"

"Correct, sir," Benny once again barked. He continued, "And Dr. Fox, what, may I ask, is the symbol of the chemical element of gold?"

"You mean, like on the periodic table?" Addison asked almost as confused as the professor had been.

"Yes, like on the periodic table," snapped Benny, really getting into this.

"Uhh, let's see, ummm... chemistry really has been a long time ago for me. Um, is it **Ag**?" she answered very unsure of herself.

"No," Charlie spoke out, "I just studied this in my chemistry class last semester. Silver is **Ag**, but gold is... **Au**." And it hit them all like a board in the forehead, but Benny had to finish his moment in the sun, "Ladies and gentlemen, I give you **How to Make Awesome Booby-traps** by **A.U. Mug**, or rather Gold-stein.

Professor Hootie was possibly more flabbergasted by Benny solving this puzzle than he was when Lizzie's back blew a giant green bubble and healed itself. He looked at Benny and asked, "How did you..."

Benny interrupted, "You people are starting to rub off on me." They both grinned.

Lizzie stood, and moved to the book they now all agreed was the "secret lever" to make the bookcase spin and reveal a hidden room. She grabbed the book, looked back at the others, smiled, gave the book a tug… and she vanished.

CHAPTER 23

THE ESCAPE

There was no spinning of the bookcase, but instead, the floor had opened up directly below Lizzie, and she had fallen straight down. The four remaining crew members were now thinking they had been wrong about which book to pull, and hoped that Lizzie's newly discovered power would protect her wherever she had fallen to.

"I knew we should have gone with <u>Treasure Island</u>," said Benny, and the others glared at him. "What?" he asked.

Then, they heard a voice, "Come on guys! What are you waiting for?" It was Lizzie's. "Get down here."

They quickly went to the edge of the hole in the floor and peered into it. It was dark and really nothing could be seen. Charlie thought it looked like a large trash chute. He was the first to climb in.

"If she can do it, then so can I," he said, and he dropped into the dark chute. He fell straight down about eight feet, then hit a solid surface, and slid in a spiral, like he was on a tall, steep corkscrew playground slide. After six turns, he dropped from the slide, landing on his feet in a room that reminded him of a hospital. Charlie now realized they had indeed picked the correct book on the bookcase.

He saw Lizzie peeking through a window in a door that was across the room. She heard him land, turned toward him, and motioned for him to come over. Before he did, he stuck his head close to the chute's opening and called out, "All clear."

He then headed over to see what Lizzie was looking at through the narrow vertical window in this metal hospital looking door. She motioned for him to stay down and out of sight, and put her index finger to her pursed lips to let him know to be quiet. He did as he was told.

He peered through the window, and was both elated and depressed by what he saw. He saw a laboratory, and he was elated that he saw both his parents alive and well, and in person. But, it upset him to see that each of them had a chain attached to one of their ankles and the other end fastened to a large pole in the center of the lab. This limited their movement like they were dogs tied to a tree in the yard.

Their parents were sitting at a long table. Both were wearing magnifying glasses and had microscopes in front of them. They were wearing white coats like they did in their dental practice back home, and they even had some dental instruments that they were using to poke at teeth.

There were two other men who were working at the other end of the table. Both of them also had chains hooked to their ankles. These men had beakers, test tubes, burners, and many colored liquids they were working with.

Then Charlie saw a large, muscular man in a black tank top and long black pants, with a sword attached to his hip. The man's skin was an aqua color, and he had a neck that must have been a foot long. He was bald except for a jet black circle of hair on the top of his head that was pulled into a pony tail with multiple rubber bands tied down the length of it. When he turned, Charlie saw a large scar running diagonally down one side of his footlong neck. He looked mean.

"Scarneck," Charlie whispered to Lizzie.

"Unless, he got that scar from a shark bite," Lizzie whispered back and smirked at him.

The others had made it down the chute, and had joined the teenagers hunkered down at the door.

"So what's the plan?" whispered Professor Hootie, directed at the Paige siblings.

"Not sure yet," said Charlie, and about that time they heard the man they assumed was Scarneck growl out, "I'll be back in half an hour, and you slugs better have today's batch ready. Goldtooth does not like waiting for his daily supplement." The man then walked out a set of swinging, double doors on the other side of the lab, which both had the same narrow, vertical window that the one they were looking through had. The doors appeared to lead to a long hallway, that again reminded Charlie of a hospital. He could see multiple doors on the side walls down the hallway, but the aqua colored man just walked straight down the long hall until he could no longer be seen.

"Well now's our chance," Lizzie said, and she opened the door to the lab.

The four prisoners immediately looked over and saw the five new arrivals. The two men working with the colorful liquids were startled and drew back in fear, but a look of joy quickly appeared on the faces of Charlie and Lizzie's parents. The two teenagers ran over and threw their arms around each of them, giving them the biggest, tightest hugs they had given since they were little children.

"I'm assuming you know these people, Edward?" said one of the men, who no longer looked frightened.

"Yes," said Dr. Edward Paige with tears in his eyes and his arms now around his daughter.

"These are our children, Charlie and Lizzie." He then looked at Charlie and Lizzie and asked, "What are you guys doing here? How did you get here? Who are these people?"

Lizzie just smiled and Charlie spoke up, "It's a long story, dad, but these are friends," he said, describing Professor Hootie, Dr. Fox, and Benny, "and the 'why we're here'… well… it's to bring mom and you home."

"Hey, what about us?" said the man who'd spoken earlier.

"Uh, yeah," responded Charlie, "I mean you guys can come, too."

"So, what's the plan?" asked their mom. "How are we going to get these things off our ankles?" she asked grabbing her chain with her hand.

"Uhhh, I'm not sure yet," said Charlie. "We don't really have all this figured out."

"Well we better figure something out quick," said their dad, "because Kyle said he'd be back in thirty minutes." Charlie and Lizzie gave each other a funny look, realizing the man they'd seen was neither Scarneck, nor Sharkbite.

"I have an idea," Benny spoke up, and all four of the lab workers were taken back that the hovering bug had spoken.

"This is Benny," stated Lizzie. "Whatcha got?"

"Let me have a crack at those locks," he said.

Mr. Paige sat down on his stool and rocked back holding the leg with the chain hooked to it into the air, and said, "Go for it."

Benny flew over and put his tiny, needle nose into the lock around Edward's ankle. He looked like a hummingbird sucking nectar from a flower. He worked his nose all around, and… *click.*

The anklet was released, and their father was free of the chain. Benny moved next to their mother's, and then to the other two men, getting faster at opening them with each one.

Once they were all free, Charlie stated, "Well, I don't suppose we can leave the same way we came in," knowing there was no way to climb up the chute they had dropped from.

"One of those doors," Edward pointed down the hallway they had seen Kyle walk down earlier, "must lead to the outside where the teeth pit is, because Kyle and Frank are always coming in with buckets of teeth. I think it's the second or third door down."

"Sounds like a plan," said Professor Hootie.

The nine of them quietly went through the swinging double doors and entered the hall. They tip-toed down to the second door. Charlie opened it and was quite surprised by what he saw. It was a room full of money. From wall to wall about four feet tall. Money from all over the universe. It wasn't stacked neatly, but instead, just piled in the floor. Charlie recognized American 1, 5, and 10 dollar bills scattered throughout the pile.

He paused for a moment at the odd room, almost forgetting that they were in such a hurry. As the others peered over his shoulder and saw what he was looking at, a narrow window, or maybe more of a door, opened high on the back wall of the room. Three fairies flew in and dove into the large pile of money, like seagulls diving for fish. They flung money around the room, like a small tornado had entered the space— coins hitting the ceiling and side walls, paper money flying into the air, and all of it falling back into the huge pile, as the three fairies dug and searched with great haste. Only a few seconds later and the chaos stopped. The fairies emerged from the pile of money. Now hovering over it, they folded the bills they had found, stuck them into the pockets of their white aprons, and flew back out the small door in the back wall, which slammed shut behind them.

"Handy-dandy," Benny stated, and the crew from the Lady Alabama laughed, but the four being rescued just looked confused.

They quickly snapped out of their brief trance, shut the door, and moved to the next one down the hall. Charlie was the first one there again, and again opened this door, which immediately was seen to lead to a stairwell that only led down.

"That's it," declared Dr. Edward Paige. "That has to be the way down to the pit."

They all raced down the stairs for five flights, and then reached the bottom and another door. Charlie, still leading the group, threw open the door, which indeed led outside. He looked up at the tall pile of baby teeth and could also see the narrow bamboo bridge they'd crossed earlier. But, with his eyes looking upward, he missed the fact that there were several metal pails at his feet. He kicked, and stumbled over them, which made a loud clanging noise that startled the others— and unbeknownst to them, the loud noise was also heard by Goldtooth's crew.

At the bottom of the pit, they saw no great way of climbing up the tall ravine wall.

"Well," stated Professor Hootie, "looks like I've got some work to do." He flew up and grabbed onto Addison's shoulders, like he'd done several times before. He flew her up to the path where they had come in and set her down near the edge of the bridge they had crossed. He then did the same with the other six Earthlings. Charlie was the last to be flown up to the bridge, and as he was set to the ground, the professor said, "Whew, this old guy is out of shape. You all start walking and I'll bring up the rear."

Addison now led the group back through the winding path of beautiful coral and white sandy ground. She was followed by the two men whom they'd rescued along with the Paiges. Then came Lizzie, Mrs. Paige, Mr. Paige, Charlie, and Professor Hootie, with Benny flying all around them keeping a look out. They walked briskly down the path, and were getting close to Goldtooth's pirate ship, when Addison turned to the man behind her, which was the oldest of the four prisoners they had rescued, and asked, "I'm curious, are you the chemist or the captain?"

The man looked slightly confused, but answered her, "I'm a chemist."

Addison then addressed the man behind him as they walked out into the opening where the pirate ship was parked, "So you're the captain?"

This man also looked confused and replied, "No, I'm a chemist, as well."

Now Addison was the one who looked confused, but before she could take another step, a voice rang out from the deck of the pirate ship, "I'm the captain!"

Chapter 24

The Showdown

They all turned toward the voice. There stood a man in a perfectly pressed all white captain's uniform, trimmed in navy, like you'd expect from the captain of a luxury cruise liner. He had a neatly shaven all white beard as well, and thus looked out of place on the pirate ship.

"Captain Slater?" stated Edward Paige obviously perplexed.

"Captain Walter Slater at your service," announced the man standing on the deck. He then put both his hands to his right eye, made a couple of maneuvers, and his right hand emerged holding a glass eyeball between his thumb and index finger.

"One-eyed Walter," stated Lizzie, and the man began to laugh wildly.

Mr. Paige started again, "Slater, you no-good, lying..." but before he could finish, a door swung open behind One-eyed Walter, hitting him in the back, which caused him to drop his glass eye on the deck of the ship. It sounded like a large marble hit the wooden floor, and it began to roll.

Walter immediately stopped laughing, dropped to the ground to try to stop the rolling orb, and cried out, "My eye, my eye, don't step on my eye."

Through the door walked seven pirates. They were all of different species. 1) There was the muscular, aqua colored Kyle with the long neck, and black ponytail. 2) Then another very muscular, mean looking creature that was tan with a flat elongated head like that of a hammerhead shark. 3) There was another sinister looking pirate whose head was football shaped. His eyes extended from his head like antenna, and when he opened his mouth, multiple rows of teeth could be seen. His skin looked like gray leather. 4) The next guy was another human, like One-eyed Walter, but this man was quite short and chubby. He had a hook replacing his right hand and a long red beard that extended all the way to the man's belly button. 5) The fifth pirate through the door was big and blue, but not it's skin— instead it was covered in fur. Well, all except its hands which they noticed only had two fingers on each. 6) The next one through the door was a female. She, like Kyle, had a long neck, but it was almost completely covered by her long, dark purple hair. Her skin was the same lavender color as Marvin, and she had three eyes; two where eyes usually are and the third where a nose usually is. 7) The last pirate who had emerged from the door was a small green fellow, only about three feet tall, yet he did not stand, but instead flew— with small wings attached to his back. His green head was shaped like that of an aardvark*, with an elongated snout, and his short little left leg was missing and in it's place was what looked like a sawed off broom stick.

They all lined up, along the deck, and tried to look as intimidating as possible. For some of them, that was easier than for others. About that time, Walter popped up from the deck's floor, and brushed off his uniform with one hand as he held his glass eye in the other. He blew onto it in order to clean it off.

The door behind him once again flew open — this time hitting Walter's elbow and sending the eyeball flying over the side of the deck and into the sand near Addison's feet. None of the crew even looked at the eye in the sand, but instead kept their gaze on the door of the ship.

The man that emerged was one that needed no introduction to the crew of the Lady Alabama. It was quite obvious who he was. With a head shaped similar to a snake's, and no upper lip, those two large teeth came through the door before he did. His skin was tan with dark brown spots, and he wore rounded golden glasses similar to the ones Professor Hootie was wearing. The gold of his glasses matched the gold of his tooth. He wore a loose, white, ruffled shirt and a classic black pirate hat, minus the feather.

When he reached the edge of the deck he peered out at the nine of them and began to speak, "I am the feared pirate captain..."

"We know who you are Vardiman," Professor Hootie interrupted.

Goldtooth was frustrated that he'd been interrupted, but also quite alarmed by this statement. "I haven't been called that in…"

"Yeah, a long time," interrupted Charlie. "Probably like 250 years or so?"

Now Goldtooth was starting to get angry. He did not like that these people seemed to know so much about him.

"What do you think you know about me?" he shouted. The other pirates, were obviously startled by his outburst.

"We know you were once a great professor at a great university," replied Professor Hootie.

"We know you kidnapped our parents to be your slaves," said Lizzie.

"We know you're using the baby teeth to stay young," stated Dr. Fox.

"And," started Charlie, "we know that if you plan to keep making that potion you're making, then you're just going to have to do it on your own."

"We'll see about that," yelled Goldtooth, and he quickly drew a revolver, which looked to be from the era of the Revolutionary War, from a holster on his hip, aimed it at Charlie, and fired before anyone even knew what he was doing.

Lizzie reacted, lunging herself toward Charlie, but she was not in time. The bullet hit him in the chest, he dropped to his knees, and then fell face first onto the sandy ground below.

"That should shut up the little brat," said Goldtooth with a smirk toward his band of pirates.

"Charlie!" yelled Lizzie.

"What have you done!?" yelled their mother, Dr. Patricia Paige.

Addison and the Paiges all rushed to Charlie on the ground.

"You should have stayed in my lab, where you belong," stated Goldtooth. "You need to accept the fact that this is your new home."

Patricia Paige glared angrily at the pirate captain while tears began to fill her eyes.

Dr. Fox began to roll Charlie over and see what could be done with his wound. At this point, the escapees had surrounded Charlie to a point that Goldtooth and his minions could no longer see him.

Dr. Fox and the Paiges, being the closest to the wounded teen, heard a faint whisper come from Charlie before they could get him rolled over. They leaned in closer and Addison asked quietly, "Charlie, can you hear me? Did you say something?"

Another whisper came back and they could barely make it out, "Just give me a second," they believed he had said.

"But Charlie, I need to see your wound, and every second counts," stated Addison.

Charlie said again, but this time quite a bit louder, "I just need a second."

Addison looked up at the members of his family as if to ask what she should do, but before anyone could give her an answer, Charlie pushed off the ground and popped back up to his feet. He wiped a slimy green substance from his chest, and appeared to be perfectly fine.

He turned to Lizzie who had a peculiar look on her face, and he said, "Don't look so surprised, sis, you had to know I drank some of the green water. I mean, I carried it in my mouth to get it to you."

Lizzie quickly retorted, "I'm not surprised... just disappointed. I wanted to be the ONLY superhero in the family."

Their parents both appeared completely perplexed, but were just happy their son was okay. Lizzie looked at her parents and said, "It's a long story."

Charlie then pushed by Professor Hootie whose body had been shielding the pirates from seeing the activities on the ground. Goldtooth was still gloating in the action he thought had defused the whole situation, when Charlie appeared from the crowd.

"You're going to have to do better than that Goldtooth," he announced to the man who'd shot him. Then, he turned to Professor Hootie and said, "Get them to the ship."

"Roger that," stated the professor, and he flew up, grabbed the older of the two chemists around the shoulders, and flew him into the air.

"Get them!" called out Goldtooth to his team, who all hurried back through the door they had emerged from earlier. All, that is, except for the winged-one they assumed to be Peg-leg Larry, who pulled out a small sword and flew toward the Professor carrying the chemist. But just as he did, Addison pulled out Jagger's laser pistol and fired a shot toward him. The shot hit Larry's wrist which caused him to drop the sword. He yelped in pain, and flew back to the deck of the pirate ship.

The other chemist and Mrs. Paige hid behind some large coral as the others prepared to fight. A door in the hull of the pirate ship opened like a drawbridge, and the band of seven pirates, now armed with various weapons, came running out toward them. Addison fired a few blasts in their direction, which scattered them like ants. They had not seen her fire the first shot at Peg-leg Larry, and were not expecting it. The chubby, red-bearded human, Hook-hand Harry, actually just dove back into the ship, and refused to come out.

The two big guys, Kyle and Frank the Plank, with his hammerhead shark looking face, came straight for Charlie. Kyle was carrying nunchucks and Frank a sword. Charlie decided not to wait, but rather to take the attack to them, and he began to sprint toward the two. They paused seeing this and prepared to swing their weapons at the teenager. Just before he got to them, Charlie leapt onto a small coral rock a foot off the ground, and used it as a sort of springboard to go into a double spinning windmill kick, which caught both the muscle-bound pirates across the face. Neither of them had landed a blow to the teen, and in fact, Kyle had lost his nunchucks in the attempt, as he took a foot to the face. Charlie landed gracefully to the ground, and right in front of him, so did Kyle's nunchucks.

Charlie quickly grabbed the nunchucks and began wielding them like the master he was. Kyle charged, and Charlie swiftly gave him another blow across the face with his own weapon. This blow rendered the big fellow unconscious, and he fell like a large oak tree to the ground.

Frank the Plank, however, had maintained possession his weapon after the kick to the face, and just as Charlie had hit Kyle, Frank slashed at the teenager from behind and sliced into his back. It stung and Charlie winced in pain, but Frank watched as the green ooze leaked from the wound, and then sealed the boy's skin back together, in a matter of seconds.

Charlie spun to face him, and said, "I dare you to do it to my face," and he began maneuvering the nunchucks again. At this point, Frank realized he was out-matched, so he dropped his sword and took off running down the path back toward the laboratory.

Meanwhile, the others were also under attack. For instance, One-eyed Walter, with a spiked club in his hand and a patch now over his eye, came charging at Edward Paige who quickly looked for something to use to defend himself. Not seeing any good options, he leaned down and scooped up something from the sand. As Walter got closer to him, Edward wound up and threw a fastball directly toward the no-good, lying cruise ship captain. (I might mention, that Dr. Edward Paige, before attending dental school, was a pitcher in Major League Baseball for the New Orleans Gators.) The object sailed through the air at approximately ninety miles per hour, and before One-eyed Walter even knew anything was coming toward him, he was hit square in the forehead by his own glass eye. He dropped like he'd been shot with a rifle.

And then there was Lizzie and Addison. Sharkbite, with his football-shaped head, came toward them carrying a mace*, a spiked ball connected to a chain. And the lavender female— they deemed to be Scarneck by process of elimination— had a crossbow with a pack of arrows strapped to her back. Addison held them off for a bit with the last pistol, and they were able to dodge the arrows from behind a large coral rock, until, all of a sudden the pistol jammed up and stopped firing. The two menacing pirates started to close in on them.

Lizzie told Addison to stay behind the rock and she sprinted toward the two of them, much like her brother had done. She leaned down and grabbed two handfuls of sand as she ran. Scarneck loaded her crossbow and fired an arrow toward Lizzie, who dodged it by doing an aerial, or no handed cartwheel. As she flew threw the air, she released the handfuls of sand which hit both the pirates right in their eyes. However, as Sharkbite was blinded by the spraying sand, his swinging spiked ball, clipped Lizzie in midair on the calf. She landed to the ground as the pain shot through her leg. She looked down at it and saw the oozing green, where blood should have been, and then the large gash just faded away and the pain went with it.

Lizzie turned around and first went to Scarneck, who was now on her knees, rubbing her three eyes, with her crossbow on the ground next to her. As Lizzie neared her, she quickly began to reach for her weapon, but Lizzie was too fast and gave her a jump kick to the face, which sent the lavender lady with dark purple hair flying to her back. Her long hair now spread all along the ground, and Lizzie could finally see her long neck, which looked like it had been a chew toy for some ferocious beast at some point in her life.

Lizzie reached down and grabbed the crossbow. She pointed it at Sharkbite, who had just gotten his vision back. "It's your call," Lizzie told him, "flee or be shot?"

The odd looking creature with the football shaped head and antenna eyes, opened his tooth-filled mouth and replied, "Goggo boggo." He then took off running down the path toward the bridge.

"I'm going to translate that as 'flee'," stated Lizzie as she turned back to face Addison.

The large, furry, blue pirate with four fingers, had kind of hung back near the ship and watched some of these happenings. Then Benny flew toward him and said, "Hey, Freddy. Don't make me come over there and put a hurtin' on you."

Four-fingered Freddy, realizing he was pretty much by himself at this point, fled the scene down the same path as Frank the Plank and Sharkbite.

While all of this was going on, Professor Hootie had returned and flown off again with the other chemist, back to the ship.

BUT, what they hadn't realized is that during all the commotion, Goldtooth had come down off the pirate ship and had grabbed Dr. Patricia Paige. When the action of the fighting stopped and Charlie, Lizzie, Edward, and Addison looked around, they saw Goldtooth with a shining, silver knife held to the throat of Mrs. Paige.

"None of you better make a move. I'm taking her back to my laboratory. The rest of you are free to go. One dentist is all I need."

"Just relax, Goldtooth," said Edward.

"You know we can't let you take our mom with you," said Charlie.

"If you try and stop me," he began as he backed toward the path they'd just come down, "then I WILL slit her… Owww!" he yelped. "My tushy! What in the world stu…?" and his voice trailed off, his body became limp, and he collapsed to the ground behind Patricia Paige.

Chapter 25

Another Race Against Time

Everyone had been caught off guard and wasn't quite sure what just happened, but Charlie had heard that yell before. He quickly rushed to where Goldtooth was lying.

Just behind Professor Vardiman Goldstein, he found Benny. He was lying almost lifeless after having transfused all his muzz into Goldtooth in a fraction of a second. With the only strength he could muster, Benny muttered two words, "My bag," and he collapsed again.

Charlie's brain, working in overdrive, remembered having seen Benny carry a small bag onto the ship back on Tropia, but he had not thought of it since. He quickly, touched his wristband and said, "Jagger, come in. We need Benny's bag. NOW!"

"Roger that," came the reply from Jagger inside the Lady Alabama.

Charlie wasn't sure what was in that bag, but he remembered from Professor Hootie's crash course on Muzz Bugs, a little over a week ago, that he only had a minute before Benny was beyond saving. And all of a sudden Charlie found himself racing against another clock. He estimated that the sting had occurred twenty seconds ago (**00:00:40**)

Addison and Lizzie rushed to Benny as well.

"Chuck?" came Jagger's voice, "do you know where he put his bag?" (**00:00:33**)

Charlie looked up at Addison and Lizzie for an answer. Addison grabbed Charlie's wrist and spoke into the band, "The side wall!" she shouted.

"It's hanging on the wall across from the co-pilot chair!" (**00:00:29**)

"Got it!" yelled back Jagger.

"I don't know that he can get it here quick enough," stated Charlie.

"We don't even know what's in the bag, do we?" asked Addison. (**00:00:21**)

"Haven't a clue," replied Charlie, "but it won't matter if we…"

Charlie was interrupted by an image soaring through the air towards them. It was Professor Hootie, and he was carrying Benny's small bag. As it had turned out, the professor had just gotten to the Lady Alabama with the second chemist when Jagger got the call from Charlie. (**00:00:13**)

Dr. Hootie dropped the bag before he'd even landed. Charlie caught it and quickly unzipped the little satchel. Inside he found hope. He found hope in the form of a syringe.

Charlie looked up at Addison and quickly said, "That's all you." **(00:00:09)**

Dr. Fox didn't hesitate, but instead reached in and pulled out the syringe whose needle was identical to the size of Benny's nose/stinger, and whose large barrel contained a light blue liquid that appeared to have tiny golden flakes, like glitter, within it. Holding the syringe in her right hand, Addison used her left hand to spread Benny's hard exoskeleton* wings slightly apart.

"Here goes nothing," she said, as she slipped the needle into the Muzz Bug's back. **(00:00:03)** And with only a single second remaining before the minute was up, she pushed in on the syringe, driving the plunger from one end of the barrel to the other, thus forcing the light blue substance into Benny.

They did not have to wait to see what happened, because Benny immediately gasped a loud breath which scared them all. In fact, it startled Addison so much she jumped back, leaving the needle dangling from Benny's back.

"That… was… NOT AWESOME!" exclaimed Benny. "And will someone get this thing out of my back?"

CHAPTER 26

LONG STORIES TOLD

They all returned to the Lady Alabama and got a warm greeting from Jagger. Benny explained that they had just witnessed the first ever muzz transfusion not through the tip of an actual Muzz Bug's nose. He said the Muzz Bugs on Tropia had been gathering the muzz from bugs who died of natural causes for years, but they had just never had the chance to see if it would actually work. They were all glad it had. Mrs. Paige especially thanked him for coming to her rescue and risking his life for hers.

The Lady Alabama lifted off the aquarium-like ground of Pollux, and as it did they saw Inger and a swarm of tooth fairies waving good-bye to them. They all waved back.

"Next stop, Earth," announced Jagger, and they were all very happy to hear this.

It was a long journey home, but the flight was filled with stories from the past couple of weeks. Charlie told his parents all about the dirt bike race he and Lizzie had had in the woods, and of her getting stung. Then how he'd met each of his friends along the way and how each had helped in their missions. He told them of their adventures in Galaxy 9, System 7 and all the various planets they had visited. Lizzie enjoyed hearing about it all again, as well.

Then Charlie told them about how scared and upset they were when they'd heard the news of the vanished cruise ship while they were visiting with Queen Lizzie in the Forest of Wimberlies. He started telling them all the leads and clues they'd followed that finally brought them to Pollux. Lizzie jumped in on much of this story telling, however. She told about all the puzzles they solved, and their narrow escape from the gillawatts on Filipany, and how she'd taken an arrow in the back for Charlie, and that they then discovered her "superpower." Charlie was quick to remind them that he'd gone four galaxies from home to save Lizzie and she'd only moved a few feet to save him, which he pointed out, "wasn't even necessary since I have the same power," he jested.

Jagger couldn't help but to jump in and tell the Paiges about Charlie's "going ninja on the Wermuth's" and the incredible obstacle course race the teenagers had won against the Okapi.

The Paiges and the two chemists were captivated by all the magnificent stories, and the Paiges hugged their children tight and told them how proud of them they were for looking after each other.

Then the Paiges told the rest of them the story of how Goldtooth's ship had appeared in Galaxy 4, and how his band of pirates robbed everyone and took them hostage. They said they never realized that Captain Slater, also known as One-eyed Walter, was in on it until they saw him on the deck of Goldtooth's ship back on Pollux. They told how they were forced to examine baby teeth all day long for Goldtooth's potion, and that until the showdown at the pirate ship, they didn't even know what the potion was for. They just knew they had to make sure none of the baby teeth used for it had any decay.

They all told about their puddle jumping experiences and how they felt the first time they did it. The Paiges said the screams on the large cruise ship were deafening during the freefall portion of their puddle jump toward Elenarrus.

Lastly, the older of the two chemists, whose name was Emmerson, told about how ten years ago he was on a science expedition in Galaxy 2, System 2 when his ship was invaded by Goldtooth and his band of pirates. He said he and another chemist on his team were taken to Goldtooth's lab, and at that time there was another dentist who was there, but that he'd been alone in the lab for about a month before the Paiges and Gary showed up.

They were almost at the end of the long journey from Galaxy 10, System 4 to Galaxy 5, System 1, and were approaching Earth's airspace, when they saw it. There she was… the huge cruise liner with the words "Saint Louis the Lionhearted" written across the side. Jagger flew the Lady Alabama over close to it, and through the window in the captain's cabin, they saw a figure in full captain's uniform, as if One-eyed Walter was driving the ship again. The captain, whose back was to them reached up and grabbed the microphone to the ship's outer speaker system. His lavender face quickly turned toward the Lady, and they heard the rhythm, "Nnt nnt nnt nnt…"

THE END

92471278R00162

Made in the USA
Columbia, SC
01 April 2018